READ ALL THE SPY KIDS™ ADVENTURES!

COMING SOON!

Based on the characters
by Robert Rodriguez

Written by Elizabeth Lenhard

HYPERION
MIRAMAX BOOKS
New York

Printed in the United States of America

First Edition

1 3 5 7 9 10 8 6 4 2

This book is set in 13/17 New Baskerville.

ISBN 0-7868-1803-4

Visit www.spykids.com

Juni Cortez ran backward across the grass in front of his family's cliff-top home.

"I got it, I got it. . . ." he called.

"It" was the Frisbee that Juni's older sister had just flung across the lawn. Juni backed up some more, his arms outstretched, waiting for the Frisbee to float down to him.

He waited.

And waited.

But the Frisbee kept flying! That's when Juni noticed a little plume of fire sputtering out of the disk. And when he glanced at his sister, he saw that she was wiggling the joystick of a tiny remote-control device.

"You slipped in a jet Frisbee?!" Juni called out. "Nice trick, Carmen. But guess what?"

"What?" Carmen called back, giggling as she steered the jet Frisbee over a gnarled oak tree.

"I have a trick up my sock, too," Juni declared.

"The correct phrase is 'trick up my sleeve,'" dork," Carmen replied.

"Not this time!" Juni announced. He bent over and rolled his sweat socks down to his sneakers. Strapped to each ankle were two tiny rockets! With the tap of a button, each rocket burst into life. Shooting jets of air over his heels, they catapulted Juni into the sky.

By now, Carmen had steered the jet Frisbee over their house. Juni flew up over the roof, did a flashy loop-de-loop and snatched the jet Frisbee out of the air. The he zinged it back to his sister on the ground and flew to the oak tree. Landing neatly on a branch, he turned off his ankle-jets and shot Carmen a smug look.

"Just remember, for every one of *your* spy gadgets, I have an equal and opposite spy gadget," Juni said to his sister. "I got your number."

"Duh," Carmen said, tossing the Frisbee on the grass and rolling her brown eyes at her bro. "We live in the same house and we're spy partners. Of *course*, you have my number."

Juni hopped down from the oak branch and ambled over to Carmen. They both sprawled on the grass and wiped beads of sweat off their foreheads.

"Correction," Juni said. "We're *off-duty* spy partners. We have an entire week of summer left. A whole, blissful week of Frisbee-playing and tadpole-catching and canoeing and stuff before OSS school starts."

The OSS was the top-secret government agency where Carmen and Juni worked. And they worked plenty hard. Between the two of them, Carmen and Juni spoke fourteen languages. In their basement workout room, they trained every day, honing their kung fu and cunning to fight off any foe. And they were constantly upgrading their arsenal of futuristic spy gadgets.

But the Spy Kids weren't total workaholics. After all, they were Spy *Kids*. Carmen was twelve and Juni was ten. They saved the world on a regular basis, but they still deserved a little summer vacation. Hence this sunshiny afternoon of jet Frisbee and lolling in the grass.

"A whole wcek before we have to think about school," Juni repeated happily. "Ahhhh! The only thing that could make this moment any better would be a big, drippy, bubble-gum ice-cream cone!"

"Carmen? Juni?"

Juni lifted his head off the grass to see their mom poking her head through the back door. As usual, Mom's green eyes were crinkled into a sweet smile. Juni propped himself up on his elbows and looked at his mother hopefully. Had she read his mind? Did she come bearing ice cream?

"Come on in, kids," Mom called.

"For a snack?" Juni asked.

"Sure," Mom agreed. "Just as soon as you try on your school uniforms and fall clothes. You know—just one more week and it's back to the books! And you guys are looking awfully lanky. I'm worried your clothes aren't going to fit."

Carmen and Juni exchanged baleful glances.

"So much for not thinking about school," Carmen sighed. Then she and Juni pulled themselves to their feet.

Even if they did complain a little, the truth was the Spy Kids weren't tremendously bummed about going back to school. After all, school—and everything else in their lives—was much cooler now that they were spies.

A few years earlier, life hadn't been nearly as exciting. Juni's classmates had teased him because he was timid and sweaty palmed. In fact, he'd been so scared, his damp hands had broken out in warts. *Blech!*

Meanwhile, Carmen had been so restless, she'd spent a lot of time moping around the house, dreaming of running away to far-off lands. She never told her parents about her discontentment. She didn't want to hurt their feelings. Besides, Carmen had thought her folks would never understand her craving for adventure. After all, they were as safe as parents could be. They worked at home as computer consultants. Mom cooked practical dinners and Dad wore sensible spectacles. Bor-ing!

But, one fateful day, Carmen and Juni found out the truth—their parents were anything but boring. In fact, once upon a time, they'd been cutthroat international superspies! But then, they'd met, fallen in love, and gotten married. And when Carmen and Juni were born, Ingrid and Gregorio had dropped out of the dangerous spy biz.

Then one day the OSS contacted Ingrid and Gregorio for one last mission. Unable to resist the adventure, the parents went off to save the world. Their mission was a breeze—until they were captured. That's when Carmen and Juni had become spies themselves and swooped in to save their parents' butts.

Now all four Cortezes spied for the OSS together. They were a lot happier, too, *even* when they had to contend with tedious stuff like trying on back-to-school clothes.

Juni went to his room and pulled his school uniform out of the closet. He tugged the outfit on and went to the kitchen where Mom and Carmen were already waiting. They took one glance at him and burst out laughing!

"What?" Juni demanded. He scowled and scratched a mosquito bite on his wrist, which was hanging well below the cuff of his burgundy blazer. "So, it's a little snug."

"Just a *little*?" Carmen giggled, pointing at her brother. "Your sleeves are three inches too short. Your shorts look like a bathing suit. And you can't even button your jacket over that roly-poly belly."

Juni glared at Carmen.

"Right back at ya," he accused.

"As if," Carmen said, skimming a hand over her slim, almost-teenage waist. "My uniform still fits."

"But what about the shoes, Bigfoot?" Juni pointed out. Carmen frowned and grabbed her school shoes off a kitchen chair. She thrust one foot into a shoe. It went as far as her third toe.

"Just as I thought," Mom said. "You kids sprouted like bean stalks this summer. We better get you some new clothes. And you know what that means."

Carmen jumped up and down, clapping her hands together.

"Shopping!" she cried. "Yes!"

"No!" Juni yelled.

"Maybe so?" said a rumbly, Spanish-accented voice in the kitchen door. "What are you kids arguing about now?"

The kids spun around. Their dad had sneaked up behind them. He was carrying his laptop in one hand and a bottle of suntan lotion in the other.

"I was just doing a little decryption work on the sundeck," he said. "But the sound of my sweet little spies getting along so nicely lured me into the kitchen."

"Ha-ha, very funny, Dad," Carmen said. "Juni doesn't want to go school-clothes shopping, of course."

"Ah, I don't blame you, son," Dad said with a grimace. "You could grow gray hair waiting for a woman to decide between this black shoe and that black shoe. It's torture!"

"Really, Gregorio?" Mom said, fixing Dad with a mischievous glare. "Torture? Like the torture you endured when you were captured by a villain during our spy mission last week? Oh, wait a minute! That baddie didn't have a chance to torture you. Because I rescued you first!"

"Very good point, my dear," Dad said quickly.

Then he muttered to Juni, "Forget I said anything. Your mother—she's a very clever lady."

"Believe me, I know," Juni said. Then his face brightened. He had an idea! Tugging off his too-tight blazer, Juni trotted over to the family computer—the one they used to surf the Web—on the kitchen desk.

"You know what they say," he said, booting up the computer. "Like mother, like son! I have a clever idea of my own. One that will get us all out of this shopping trip!"

"Juni . . ." Mom chided him.

"Just wait till you see this awesome site before you say anything," Juni begged. So Mom—and Carmen—folded their arms over their chests and waited as Juni pointed and clicked his way to a particular Web site. Suddenly, the computer screen erupted with crazy colors, pulsing cartoon shopping carts, and bright dollar bills. Jingly music echoed out of the speakers. Then a man's face popped up in the center of the screen. He had slick, yellow, overstyled hair, a jutting jaw with a cleft chin, and sparkly blue eyes. He began rattling off a lightning-fast sales pitch.

"Something that slices and dices?" he proposed. "How 'bout some mices? The duds that are nicest?

Cures for your vices! Buy them ALL for low, low, looooow prices at Whoppershopper.com."

Mom gave Juni a dry look.

"Nice try, sweetie," she said, "but we're going to the real mall."

"But . . . but . . . look how cool this site is," Juni protested. "No dressing rooms. No tromping around from store to store. And you can still try on stuff. See?"

Juni hit a few computer keys. Then he jumped out of his chair and onto a hexagonal pad on the floor next to the desk.

"Careful with that teleportation pad," Dad cautioned his son. "You know your Uncle Machete made it. You don't want to end up beaming yourself to China!"

Carmen and Juni giggled. Dad's brother, Machete Cortez, was the most creative gadget inventor in the history of the OSS. But sometimes Uncle Machete was a little *too* creative. His watermelon-seed blowgun, for instance, worked fine— if you didn't mind the flatulent noises it made with every shot. His Chameleo-Candy helped the kids blend seamlessly into any environment. Unfortunately, it also tasted like freeze-dried lizards. And his teleportation pad? Well, it was still a bit crude. But, at the moment, Juni had confidence.

"I'm not going anywhere," he assured his dad. "That's the point. The clothes come to you!"

And he was right. Just then, an electronic voice rang out from Whoppershopper.com: "Now teleporting outfit #256—the Radical Skate Kid."

A flash of light filled the kitchen. When the Cortezes blinked the spots out of their eyes, Juni was no longer wearing his supersnug school uniform. Instead, he was dressed in the baggiest, most billowing cargo pants ever. *And* the skimpiest, most garishly colored T-shirt ever. On one foot was a green suede sneaker, size 12. On the other was a red high-top, size 6.

"Okay, so maybe there are still a few glitches in the system," Juni said, shrugging at his awestruck family. "But that's okay. We can tweak it. This outfit isn't real. It's virtual. You can try on clothes without really trying them on."

"It brings a whole new meaning to the term 'mix and match,'" Mom said with a laugh. "I'm sorry, sweetie. But we really need to get you clothes that fit and that means we're *going* to the mall."

"Even I have to agree with your mother on that one," Dad said, clapping an apologetic hand on

Juni's shoulder. "No Cortez can go out in public looking this uncool."

"Whoo-hoo!" Carmen cried. She headed for the kitchen door. "Time to shop till we drop. I'm going to put on some glittery eye shadow before we go."

Ah-WHOOP! Ah-WHOOP! Ah-WHOOP!

"Hold your horses, shop girl!" Juni cried gleefully. "That's the OSS alarm! It's mission time! And you know what that means. We won't be going anywhere near a mall today!"

Suddenly, Juni lurched forward.

"Whoa!" he yelled.

Something had forced him off the teleportation pad! When he found his balance, he spun around. The virtual image of a broad-shouldered, cleft-chinned man had taken his place on the pad.

"Mr. Devlin!" Juni cried.

"Hello," Devlin said with a wave to the family. He was the head of the OSS and a very important man—which was why Juni and Carmen had to work extra hard to stifle their giggles at his appearance. Now that he was standing on the teleportation pad instead of Juni, he was wearing Juni's ridiculous skater-kid outfit, two different shoes and all!

Luckily, Devlin himself didn't notice his bright-

and-baggy getup. He was too intent on giving the spy family their next mission.

"Cortezes," he announced. "Break out your credit cards. You're going to the mall!"

CHAPTER 2

"**W**e're going where?" Juni gasped.

His boss grinned.

"The mall," Devlin said. "Kids love the mall! So I figured you wouldn't mind cutting your summer vacation a little short for this mission."

"Well . . ." Juni began, but Carmen cut him off with an elbow to the ribs.

"We don't mind at all, Mr. Devlin," she blurted. "The OSS comes first, of course! Now, you were saying? Y'know, about the . . . mall?"

Carmen's eyes glittered with excitement. A mission at a mall! This was a dream come true!

"Well, this isn't just any mall," Devlin explained. "We're sending you to the Mall of the Universe."

"Get out!" Carmen cried in delight. Then she remembered that she was addressing the head of the OSS. "I mean, get out, sir."

"At ease, Spy Kid," Devlin said with one rakish wink. "I take it you've heard of the Mall of the

Universe then. What teenager hasn't? It's the world's largest mall, covering eight square miles of North Dakota flatlands. This mall has got it all—an indoor amusement park and water slide, countless food courts and movie theaters, a skateboarding ramp, glass people movers on monorails, a rock-climbing wall, and, oh, I almost forgot, hundreds and hundreds of stores."

"So what's our mission? Tracking down a super-shoplifter?" Juni asked with an arched eyebrow. "What'd he take? Jewels? Clothes? The special recipe for the Whopper."

"Try the entire mall," Devlin said with a sigh.

"What?!" the spy family gasped.

"Devlin, my hearing must be a little faulty," Dad said. "Are you telling us that someone has made off with an eight-square-mile building?"

"In a manner of speaking," the chief replied. "Our villain—whose identity is still unknown—has cloaked the entire mall in a virtual environment."

"So the Mall of the Universe has become an *alternate* universe?" Juni said.

"Exactly," Devlin said. "And whoever was shopping when the virtual environment was activated is trapped inside. Where there were once harmless shops and restaurants, there is now a cartoonish prison.

"Our satellite surveillance," he continued, "has given us just a glimpse of this horrible anti-mall. Have you heard of Dante's inferno—the nine circles of, ahem, heck? Well, picture Dante as a Valley girl and you'll have a notion of what we're dealing with. There are escalators that go on forever. Roller coasters that crawl instead of coast. Perfume spritzers who've gone mad, forcing shoppers to submit to humiliating makeovers. And others are being pelted with popcorn and kneaded into gigantic cinnamon rolls."

"Well, *that* doesn't sound so bad," Juni said, licking his lips.

Carmen rolled her eyes at her ever-hungry brother, then turned back to their badly dressed boss.

"I know this computer program," she said. "The virtual environment is bordered by invisible walls—a sort of electric fence. The shoppers were probably tagged with something that's now keeping them inside those walls."

"And, since you Cortezes haven't been tagged, you could theoretically penetrate these barriers?" Devlin asked eagerly. "That's key. Because we're sure that the villain is running his program from somewhere inside the virtual mall."

"You're right about that," Carmen said, biting her lower lip. "But I doubt we can just waltz through the virtual walls. That would be too easy. The villain must have put up some blockers. But, Devlin, how big did you say the Mall of the Universe was?"

"Eight square miles," Devlin replied. "Ugh! Can you imagine shopping for eight square miles?"

"No!" Juni and Dad blurted.

"Sure!" Carmen said at the same moment. "But actually, that's not why I asked. If our villain has covered that much mileage, there must be seams in the cloak."

"Uh, translation, please?" Juni said.

"There's no computer in the world strong enough to create such a huge, seamless environment," Carmen explained. "It just isn't possible. So, this madman must have created cells layered next to one another—sort of like hexagons in a honeycomb."

"Uh-huh," Devlin, Juni, Mom, and Dad said blankly.

"Between each cell," Carmen explained patiently, "there's got to be a seam—a sliver of space that's *non*virtual. And *that's* where we get in."

"Thank goodness there is a way in," Devlin

breathed. "Like I said, the computer program running this inferno is inside the inferno itself. Saving the shoppers means penetrating the virtual barriers, finding the computer hub, and dismantling the program. Carmen—you're the best hacker in the OSS. So, you're our man . . . uh . . . girl."

"Thanks," Carmen said. "But I don't usually do solo missions, Mr. Devlin."

"Oh, believe me, this mission is going to require every last Cortez," Devlin said. "Between navigating the crazy mall, tracking down the computer, and catching the villain, you'll have your hands full!"

"Well, Dad," Juni said, turning to his father with a sigh. "I guess we're going to the mall after all."

"Perfect," Devlin said. "Normally, we'd fly you to North Dakota on an OSS hyperspeed jet. But we're assuming the madman has outfitted the mall with satellite surveillance. We don't want to tip him off to the presence of spies."

"Of course," Juni said.

"So, you'll fly on a commercial flight leaving in forty-five minutes," Devlin said. "There will be an OSS car waiting for you at the airport. Then just follow the signs to the Mall of the Universe. It's the biggest tourist attraction in the state. You really can't miss the place. Oh, and Cortezes?"

"Yes, sir?" Dad said.

"Pick me up a new shirt when the mission's completed, won't you?" Devlin said, glancing down at his ridiculous skater t-shirt. "This is *no* way for the OSS chief to be dressed."

A few hours later, the Cortezes were driving through the flatlands of North Dakota. Dad was at the wheel, and Mom was navigating.

"Oh, look, honey," Mom said, pointing at an enormous, sparkly sign along the highway. "Devlin was right. We just follow these billboards. This one says, 'Just 10.3 miles to the Mall of the Universe, the biggest mall in the Universe. You betcha!'"

Carmen giggled. About thirty seconds later, she pointed out the window and cried, "There's another one! 'Just 10.1 miles to the Mall of the Universe.'"

"'Golly,'" Juni read a few seconds later. "'Only 9.8 miles to the Mall of the Universe.' Gee, I can't wait."

"These folks sure are enthusiastic!" Mom said brightly after the Cortezes had driven past about a dozen more breathless MOTU signs.

"Friendly, too!" Carmen pointed out as Dad turned into the MOTU parking lot.

"Imagine how grateful they will be," Dad said,

driving down a parking lot aisle, "when we save the day for the—hey! Did you see that?"

Dad had been just about to pull into a choice parking space right near the mall entrance. But before he could even turn the steering wheel, a minivan screeched down the aisle and swooped in to steal the spot.

The mom driving the minivan poked her head through her car window and cackled, "You snooze, you lose, out-of-towner!"

Dad sputtered, "Of all the rude, rotten . . ."

"Honey," Mom said, "don't pay any attention. There's a spot up ahead."

Shaking his head, Dad steered the OSS car toward the parking space Mom had pointed out. This time, some kids on zippy motor scooters swerved into the space just ahead of him. They were playing their music so loud, they couldn't hear Dad's protests.

"Why don't we just go over there to park?" Carmen said. She was pointing to the far reaches of the parking lot, about three quarters of a mile from the entrance.

"And walk all that way?" Dad sputtered. "This is America! It just isn't *done*. I will find us the perfect parking space."

Mom glanced at Carmen, who looked bewildered.

"The quest for the perfect parking space," Mom whispered dryly. "It's a guy thing."

"Yeah, and meanwhile, our mission is going cold," Carmen hissed back. "How are we going to save the world if we can't even park the car?!"

CHAPTER 3

"**Y**ou see," Juni sighed a few minutes later. Dad had just circled the Mall of the Universe parking lot for the tenth time. "*This* is why all malls are evil. Dad's completely lost it!"

"Silly SUV . . ." Dad was grumbling. "M*y* parking space . . . North Dakota . . . Grrrrr." Dad's knuckles were white. His black, wavy hair was sticking up all over his head. And his eyes had a crazed glint to them.

"You're right," Carmen said to Juni. "I haven't seen him this worked up since the neighborhood bully stole your baseball bat. He's gone all *crazy-dad* on us."

"Happens to the best of them," Mom agreed with a weary nod.

"But aren't we forgetting something?" Juni said, bracing himself against his car door as Dad swerved angrily into yet another parking lot lane. "This isn't just any dad! And this isn't just any car!"

With that, Juni reached into the front seat and scanned the dashboard. In addition to the usual air conditioner, windshield wiper, and radio controls, Juni saw a few OSS extras—a robotic backseat driver, a milk shake machine, and turbo rocket boosters.

Mmmmm, milk shake, Juni thought dreamily. But then he shook himself out of his snack daydreams. The mission came first. He reached out and jabbed the turborocket button.

Fwoooom!

"Whooaaaaa!" Dad cried in a very unspylike manner. The sleek, silver OSS car had suddenly jumped ten feet into the air. It began skimming swiftly over the countless cars in the mall parking lot. Dad quickly recovered his wits and began steering the flying car.

"Thanks, son," he sighed. "I needed that. Don't know what came over m—aha!"

Dad suddenly forgot what he was saying. He'd spotted something—a car pulling out of the best space in the whole lot! The spot was extra wide and placed near the front of the lane. It was a mere twenty feet from the mall's main entrance. A parking spot like that came along once in a lifetime!

And Dad wasn't the only one who'd seen it. A

station wagon filled with kids was zipping straight toward the spot.

"Oh, no, you don't," Dad yelled. "That spot is mine!" He hit the gas pedal so hard the turborockets spewed yellow sparks. Then he sent the car into a nosedive.

"Aaaaaahhh!" Mom, Carmen, and Juni shrieked.

Thuunnk!

The OSS car landed loudly in the spot, cutting the station wagon off cold. The mom behind the wheel shook her fist at Dad, then sped off in a huff.

"Ladies and gentleman," Dad announced smugly. "I have parked the car! What would you have done without your Papi, eh?"

"Um, parked where I suggested and used our jetpacks to zip to the mall entrance?" Carmen said brightly.

"Ahem, well, I suppose that was an option, too," Dad said sheepishly. "But where's the challenge?"

"Coming right up!" Juni answered. He pointed through the car window at the mall entrance.

"Um, that is a good point, too, my boy," Dad said, looking even more sheepish.

Mom patted Dad on the shoulder and shot him a forgiving grin. Then she turned around to gaze seriously at the Spy Kids.

"Okay, mission time!" she said. "Does everyone have their gear?"

"Roger," Carmen said grimly.

"Roger," Juni said right after.

The Cortezes pulled out billowing, mesh shopping bags. Each bag was stocked with gadgetry, from shooting cables for swinging from the mall's mezzanine to fluorescent-light-channeling solar guns.

"Okay," Juni said, hopping out of the car. "Let's do this."

"Carmen, you focus on locating the computer hub," Mom instructed as the spies walked toward the mall door. "We'll back you up. And kids, remember—in a virtual environment, anything is possible. This mall is definitely going to be a bit bizarre. . . ."

Mom's voice trailed off as they walked through the door. They looked around with wide eyes. Carmen gasped. And Juni gaped!

They were looking at . . . the least bizarre mall they'd ever seen! It was silent, but for the hum of the dimmed, fluorescent lights. Nearby, a candy store, a bubble-bath shop, and a women's clothing boutique—though empty—looked perfectly normal.

Juni looked around in exasperation.

"Okay, first there was the annoying parking lot, and now there are a lot of boring stores," he complained. "Looks like an average American mall."

Juni began to amble down the wide corridor between the stores. As Carmen watched him, she got a funny feeling in her gut. Her spy instincts were kicking in. She just *knew* there was something fishy about this very nonfishy setting.

"Juni," she began. "Don't make another move! This could be a trap—"

Squelch!

Before Carmen could complete her warning, Juni disappeared in midstep!

"Juni!" Mom cried. Then she glanced at her daughter and husband. All together, the spies exclaimed, "A seam!"

"Juni must have passed through one of the barriers into the virtual mall," Carmen cried. "Let's go!"

Joining hands, the three remaining spies ran toward the exact spot where Juni had evaporated.

Squelch. Squelch. SQUELCH!

Carmen cringed as she passed through the seam. It felt as disgusting as it sounded—like cold, jiggly slime. When she'd squeezed completely through, she looked down at herself. She expected her cool spy outfit—black cargo pants, a long-sleeved, yellow OSS shirt, and a gizmo-laden utility belt—to be smeared with gross goo. But she blinked in surprise. Her clothes weren't be-smirched in the least!

Then Carmen blinked again. And again. And she shook her head, which was suddenly feeling quite dizzy.

When Carmen looked up, she saw why. Her clothes might have survived the journey into the virtual mall, but everything else around her had gone nuts!

To begin with, the Cortezes had landed right on the merry-go-round. Except this was no sweet little kid's ride. The carousel was spinning at an alarming rate. Carmen clung to one of the poles for support. Then she recoiled. Attached to the pole was not a pretty, painted wooden horse, but a garish, fiberglass clown. Its shiny, enormous face leered at Carmen tauntingly. Then it unleashed an earsplitting cackle. As if clowns weren't scary enough already!

Gazing around the carousel, Carmen saw Juni, Mom, and Dad. They were each clinging to poles of their own. Every time one of them struggled to move to a different part of the carousel, a virtual cartoon character would pop up to block the path. The cartoons pulsed with bright neon colors, shrieking and jiggling.

Squinting past these virtual creatures, Carmen could just make out the surroundings beyond the merry-go-round. Bizarre didn't begin to describe them.

The entrance to every store had become a pulsing, terrifying mouth. A coin fountain in the middle of one of the many mall courtyards seemed to be spewing hot lava. The steps of the endless escalator popped up at random intervals, throwing shoppers over the rails. They landed on a bobbling moonwalk that jiggled them until they looked absolutely green.

Speaking of . . . Carmen was starting to feel pretty queasy herself. Painfully, she pulled herself over to Juni, who was doing his best to kung fu chop one of the obnoxious cartoon characters. He would have taken the critter out if it hadn't been completely virtual. When Juni touched it, it disappeared with a poof and a deafening giggle.

"We've gotta get off this thing," Juni yelled to his sister through gritted teeth. "This is no merry-go-round. It's a merry-too-*loud*."

"No kidding," Carmen yelled back. "Earsplitting

and totally obnoxious. But it's moving too fast to just jump off. We have to stop it somehow."

"How?!" Juni screamed.

Before Carmen could wonder out loud, she saw a glint in her peripheral vision. She turned toward the center of the merry-too-loud and strained to focus through the tremendous noise and bright colors. There! She saw it again. Sticking out of the carousel's central post was a shiny, brass ring. Carmen knew that on an ordinary merry-go-round, snagging that ring won you a prize.

Who knows what the merry-too-loud's ring is going to do, Carmen thought with a grimace. But *anything* would be better than just clinging to this whirligig.

So she just had to figure out how to grab the ring.

She reached into her shopping bag and pulled out an extra large, extra stretchy rubber band. Once upon a time, Uncle Machete had told the Spy Kids never to leave home without a rubber band— it was a million gadgets in one.

"Let's just hope he was right," Carmen muttered. Efficiently tying a couple of sailor's knots in the band, she strung it between two of the merry-too-loud's poles. Then she pressed the small of her back into the rubber band and took a few steps backward.

The rubber band stretched taut. Carmen inched back some more. And more. Finally, the rubber band had reached its limit. It would not stretch anymore.

"What are you doing?" Juni yelled at Carmen. "If you want to slingshot yourself off this thing, you're facing the wrong way."

"And leave you guys behind to hog all the fun?" Carmen shouted with a wink. She turned back to focus on the ring. She did a quick physics calculation in her head. Then she crossed her fingers and, at precisely the right time, she lifted her feet from the floor.

Sproiiinnngg!

"Aaaaah!" Carmen cried as she sailed toward the merry-too-loud's central shaft. She barely missed three poles before she collided with the carousel's center and—the brass ring!

Triumphantly, Carmen yanked the ring off the little hook in the merry-too-loud's middle. Then she held her breath to see what would happen.

The results were *not* good.

The merry-too-loud got louder.

And then it spun harder.

It began to become unbalanced, bobbling up and down on its axis, shaking the spies like popcorn kernels. Finally, it began to spin so fast they couldn't hold onto their poles any longer. They went careening through the air!

"Aaaaaaaah!" screamed every last Cortez.

And where we'll land, nobody knows, Carmen thought in guilty panic as the spy family hurtled through the air.

Squelch! Squelch! Squelch! Squelch!

"Ooof!" Juni grunted as he landed on the floor. Nearby, Carmen, Mom, and Dad were also skidding to a halt on their butts. They looked as dazed as Juni felt.

"The next time I beg you to take me to an amusement park," Juni groaned to his parents, "please say no."

"Ditto on the mall," Carmen moaned, holding her temples. Then she looked around.

"Hey, it looks like the merry-too-loud tossed us right back to where we started," she said. All evidence of the horrible virtual mall had disappeared. Once again, the Cortezes were stranded in the actual—and thoroughly quiet—mall.

Juni lurched woozily to his feet and stumbled back to the spot where the spies had squelched through the invisible wall. There was no trace of the virtual inferno. Frowning, Juni began waving his hands through the air and poking his fingers out in front of him. Finally, one of his pokes opened a shimmery hole in the invisible wall! The edges of the hole undulated like the body of a delicate jellyfish.

And through the hole, Juni and his family could see straight into the virtual mall. The carousel was still spinning loudly. A giant candy machine was shooting gum balls in every direction. Earsplitting elevator music played on the sound system. It was distorted so it sounded even more unbearable than usual.

And the shoppers were freaking out. They ducked the gum balls with anxious shrieks. They cowered beneath the umbrella tables in a nearby food court (until, of course, the huge umbrellas began snapping at them like Venus's-flytraps). They were all definitely in need of saving—all of them, that is, except for three kids in graduating sizes who were coming straight for the fluttery hole in the wall.

They look totally on top of things, Juni thought. He smiled and waved to the kids—two boys and a girl. They waved back and trotted over to them, stopping several feet away.

"Dude," said the tallest boy. "That was a killer

splat off the merry-go-round. You guys looked just like my favorite video game, Super-Squashed Paratroopers IX."

"Well, I guess that makes sense," Juni said with a shrug. "We're here from the OSS."

"Kewl!" the older boy said. "I'm Jake, by the way."

"Hi, Jake," said Carmen. She'd silently sidled up next to her brother. Juni watched her take in Jake's sporty clothes, his long-lashed blue eyes, and the blond hair spiking out from beneath his baseball cap. Then he saw her face go all red and flirty.

Oh, man, Juni thought with a huff. Make way for another Carmen crush. Girls! They always dig the skater punks!

"I'm Carmen," Juni's swoony sister said.

"Kewl," Jake said again. Then, he jerked his thumb toward his companions. The movement made the gear strapped to the belt loops of his low-slung skater shorts jangle. The guy was outfitted with a cell phone, pager, Game Boy, Walkman TV— the works.

"This squirt is my little brother, Mickey," he said, bopping a grinning, bespectacled little boy on the head. "He's seven."

"Gunngh!" Mickey said with a little wave. His

mouth was full of some sort of mongo snack. It looked like a lime green corn dog.

Clearly, Juni thought, the snacks have gone bizarro, too. Still looks tasty, though.

"And this is Pollyanna," Jake said, pointing to the girl in the group. She glared at Jake.

"*What*-ever," she muttered. Then she shifted a bright red wad of bubble gum from her right cheek to her left and addressed the Spy Kids directly.

"My name is *not* Pollyanna," she said. "Well, actually it is. My parents went through a Hayley Mills phase right before I was born. But nobody calls me that. I'm Red, see?"

She twirled one of her brown pigtails. It was laced with fire-engine-red hair extensions. Her sequined Hello Kitty T-shirt was candy-apple red. Her superflared bootlegs were embroidered with cherry-colored flowers. And her *très* trendy suede boots were red, too.

"I'm Jake's best friend," Red went on. "Even though I'm eleven and he's thirteen. That's 'cuz girls mature faster. Plus, I'm supersmart and I skipped a grade. Some people think Jake's just pretending to be my best friend? Because my sister's, like, seventeen and can drive us to the mall every day? But that's so not true, right, Jake?"

"Dude, not true at all," Jake said with a gruff grin. To prove it, he gave Red a friendly punch on the arm.

"Man, it's a good thing your sister didn't stay at the mall today," Mickey piped up, wiping some blue mustard off his upper lip. "She'd be wigging if she was here."

"Uh, speaking of wigging," Juni said, "can you tell us what's been happening?"

"Please do," Mom said. She and Dad strode over to stand behind Carmen and Juni at the window. "We're Carmen and Juni's parents."

"A real whole spy family?" Jake breathed. "Keeeewlll!"

"Heeeehh," Carmen giggled weakly.

"That's right," Dad said. "We are the Cortezes, OSS Spy Family. And we're going to get you out of this. So do not be afraid, okay, Jake?"

"Daaaadd," Carmen muttered through gritted teeth. She squirmed in embarrassment. "Does he *look* scared to you? He's kewl as a cucumber."

"Well, we were freaked at first," Jake admitted. "But once we figured out what happened, we were okay with it. It's, like, the mall went all matrix on us."

"Yeah, and now we're trapped here," Red said.

She held up her wrist and showed the spies a tight, yellow bracelet with the silvery letters "MOTU" emblazoned on it.

"What's that?" Juni asked, eyeing identical bracelets on Jake's and Mickey's wrists.

"It's a Mall of the Universe promotional bracelet," Red said. "These mall workers were strapping one on to every shopper who came in."

"We thought it was, like, fashion," Mickey cut in. "But actually, they're more like those zappy dog collars. You know, the kind that gives Spot a shock if he tries to jump the electric fence?"

"Harsh!" Juni said.

"Tscha!" Red agreed. "You try to break through the cloaking system with one these things on and it's 'Shock it to me, baby!'"

"One guy tried it," Jake said with a sorrowful nod. "The minute he hit the wall, he started smokin'! We had to douse him with the fro-yo machine."

The spies exchanged troubled glances.

"They were tagged," Carmen said. "I knew it! Luckily, they missed us!"

"And we have our entryway," Dad said, pointing to the shimmery hole in the cloak. "So, are you ready to go back into this mall of madness and save the day?"

"Ready!" the other spies shouted. They piled their hands on top of one another's in solidarity.

"I will go first," Dad announced heroically, backing away from the hole. "Stand back, children."

Dad began running toward the hole. After three precisely spaced steps, he made his leap. As he soared through the air, he thrust his hands over his head.

Next he'll plunge through the hole and somersault to his feet, Juni thought proudly. Our dad's pretty kewl, I gotta admit.

Klaaanggg!

"Ay-yai-yai!" Dad shrieked.

His head had hit the hole in the barrier as if it were a cast-iron skillet! Dad was blocked cold. And a moment later, he was *out* cold!

"Gregorio," Mom cried, leaping to his side. Reaching into her mesh shopping bag, she pulled out a small red capsule and broke it beneath her husband's nose. Instantly, Dad awoke, sputtering and snorting and—sobbing!

"Dude, those are some strong smelling salts!" Jake said from his side of the seam.

"Custom-made by Uncle Machete," Mom said with a nod. "Hot chilies, chocolate, and the smell of Grandma Cortez's paella. It gets him every time. My husband is . . ."

". . . very emotional," both Carmen and Juni announced with a giggle.

"And very bummin'!" Jake added. "How are you guys gonna get in here now?"

Carmen eyed the shimmery hole. She walked up it and rapped it with her fist. Then she struck it harder. Little red and orange sparks shot out from beneath her knuckles.

"Just as I suspected," Carmen said. "Our villain installed an emergency fire wall. It'll pop up every time the cloak is breached. If we're going to get in there, we've got to start from scratch and find ourselves a new seam in the virtual barrier."

"Whoa," Jake said, gazing at Carmen in awe and chagrin. "*Un*-kewl."

"**O**kay, so we've gotta boogie," Juni told the mall rats. "We're going to find a way in there and save you guys. Spread the word to the other shoppers. But whatever you do, stay under the radar."

"You go, Spy Kids," Mickey cried, jumping up and down and punching his skinny arms into the air. "And, uh, you too, Spy Parents."

"*Gracias*," Dad said. He started to back away from the window. "But, please," he said, "be careful, children."

Mom and Juni started off after Dad. They had a lot of ground to cover if they were going to find another seam. The mall was enormous. It could be anywhere!

Carmen trailed behind her family, shooting one last longing glance back at Jake. He waved at her again, looking a little wan himself. Suddenly, his face lit up.

"Hey, Carmen!" he called. "I just thought of

something. Do you *have* to be a spy to help take out this dork?"

Carmen blinked in surprise. Why hadn't she thought of that earlier!? The Cortezes were outside the virtual mall, but Jake, Red, and Mickey were *in*. They could totally help with the mission. Carmen trotted back to the window. She looked through the seam at Jake.

"There *might* be something you can do," she said with a smile. "But you have to promise me you won't put yourselves in any danger."

"Sure," Jake said with a shrug. "I'm not looking for trouble. But anything would be better than just sitting around the food court, watching Mickey eat."

"Hey, speak for yourself," Mickey protested. He'd just pulled a bag of orange candied nuts out of his baggy jeans pocket and was busy munching away.

Meanwhile, Carmen was thinking.

"The only thing I know for sure about this computer program," Carmen told the mall rats, "is it's huge. We're talking mega RAM. And that means, it requires a ton of electricity to keep the computer up and running."

"Yeah?" Red said.

"So, there's a chance that all that energy might drain wattage from nearby areas," Carmen said. "Maybe you could search the mall for signs of a power drain—you know, dimmed lights or weird sparks. Power-outs. Anything unusual." Carmen looked at Jake. "Jake, does your cell phone work in there?"

"Of course," Jake said, unclipping his tiny, electric blue phone from his belt and showing it to Carmen. "I've got the latest tech."

"Okay, just call me on my spy watch if you see anything," Carmen said. She held out her wrist to show the kids her watch. It was large and glinty and capable of just about anything, from satellite-assisted navigation to wireless communication to computer hacking. Carmen and Juni never went anywhere without their spy watches.

"Whoa!" Jakc said, peering at the gadget. "I guess I don't have the *very* latest tech. That's the kewlest thing I ever saw."

Carmen felt herself blushing. Then she gave her head a little shake.

Hello, Carmen? She told herself. Mission time? Hundreds of lives and shopping establishments at stake? Get ahold of yourself, Cortez.

Carmen rattled off her spy watch's contact

number to Jake, who keyed it into his cell phone's memory bank. Then he pulled a brown paper bag out of his baggy shorts pocket.

"I picked this stuff up from Pincher's Gifts," he said. "They're just gags that have gone all wacky in the virtual mall. But who knows, maybe they'll come in handy. I copped tons of them, so why don't you have these."

Jake winged the bag through the hole. It landed, smoking slightly, at Carmen's feet. She picked it up and slipped the packet into her mesh shopping bag.

"Thanks," Carmen said. She felt a gushy smile crinkle up her face. So much for keeping cool. "And good luck."

She dashed off to find her family. She didn't have to search long. Only a few hundred feet down the dimmed mall corridor, they'd found another seam!

Or rather it had found them!

Carmen gasped.

This portal was no mere hole. Like the mawlike storefronts in the virtual mall, the seam had taken on the shape of a snout—complete with a giant, toothy mouth! It was almost transparent. Carmen could barely make out the snout's silvery outlines as it lunged out of the invisible wall. It growled and snapped at the spies. And then, it snagged one of them—Juni!

"Get it off me!" Juni began screaming.

The mouth had seized him by the feet and was gnawing on him like he was a giant lollipop! Mom and Dad leaped toward their son, but when they tried to pull him out of the hole, several more almost invisible snouts erupted from the wall and snapped at *them.*

"Hang on, Juni!" Mom cried. She had just dumped her shopping bag of gadgets onto the floor and begun pawing through them. "We'll save you. As soon as we figure out how!"

"That's not very reassuring," Juni yelled back.

"This is all being orchestrated by the villain's computer," Mom said to Dad and Carmen. "If only we could hack our way out of this!"

"Impossible," Dad said through gritted teeth. "The computer—and the madman who pro-grammed it—are in *there!*"

He gestured angrily at the invisible wall.

"So we come up with Plan B," Carmen cried. "We'll . . . we'll . . ."

Carmen was racking her brains for a rescue plan when a voice distracted her.

The voice was bellowing angry phrases.

And cackling madly.

And getting closer!

Carmen dropped into a kung fu fighting stance. She raised her fists and planted her feet. Her eyes narrowed into highly focused slits. Their invader was coming into view!

He ran down the mall corridor toward the Cortezes. His big, jiggly belly bounced a foot in front of him, and his frizzy shock of brown curls bounced, too. He was wearing a tattered brown uniform that looked vaguely military.

In one plump hand, he held a spindly wooden chair. And in the other, he had a long, brown, leather whip.

"Hold it right there!" Carmen barked.

"Yeah!" Mom and Dad said, planting themselves behind their daughter.

"Sorry, no time!" the man huffed. "Gotta rescue this poor kid over here!"

And then, as Carmen and her parents looked on in shock, the man hustled over to the virtual mouths.

"Yah, yah!" the man shouted. He cracked his whip at one of the silvery snouts like a professional lion tamer.

It worked! Instantly, the mouth whimpered and retracted back into the virtual wall, finally disappearing from view entirely.

"It's the noise these chewbabies hate," the man said over his shoulder as he cracked the whip again. "They're big scaredy-cats, really."

"Well, if it's noise they want, noise they'll get," Carmen said with determination. While the man continued to fend off the snouts with cracks of his whip, Carmen thrust her hand into her shopping bag. She pulled out the paper parcel Jake had given her and quickly glanced through the assorted gifts.

"Aha," she said, snatching up one of the items. "Looks like this cherry bomb has been virtualized into a cherry *tree* bomb. Five hundred times the noise."

She focused a searing laser beam from her spy watch onto the cherry tree bomb's fuse. The little wick quickly began sputtering and sparking.

"Everyone," she ordered. "Cover your ears!"

Carmen tossed the cherry tree bomb over toward Juni. It landed next to his elbow.

BOOOOOMMMMMM!

The noisemaker exploded with such force, the

entire mall seemed to tremble. The spies and the strange man were wetly pelted with scads of maraschino cherries.

But more importantly, the remaining virtual snouts screeched and retreated back into their invisible wall. Juni's feet suddenly came back into view. He rolled away from the virtual barrier and wiggled his limbs happily.

"Sweet!" he said, savoring his freedom. Then he picked a few splatted cherries off his shirt and popped them into his mouth. "Literally! Great gadget, Carmen!"

Mom ran to embrace Juni in a bear hug. Then, she turned to the rest of the group.

"Juni's right, sweetie," Mom said to her daughter. "Great save! But we also owe this nice man."

Mom extended her hand to the stranger.

"How can we thank you, Mister . . .?"

"Pichman," the man said, shaking Mom's hand wearily. "Webster D.C. Pichman. Head of security here at the Mall of the Universe. You must be shoppers. How did you manage to escape?"

"Shoppers?" Juni blurted. "No way. We're spies. We're here to save the day."

"Oh!" Webster said. His friendly face suddenly deflated a bit. "Save the day. How . . . wonderful."

Dad strode up to the man and clapped a friendly arm around his shoulders.

"I know what you're thinking," Dad said sympathetically. "You're the head of security. You would like to save the day all by yourself. But, believe me, there's no shame in needing a little help from the OSS. Whoever has taken over this mall is a genius. An evil, mad genius. There's no way you could have seen this takeover coming."

While Webster nodded appreciatively, Juni scrutinized the security officer.

"Do I know you from somewhere?" Juni asked. "You look really familiar."

"Oh, I get that all the time," Webster said. "You know those 'You are Here' kiosks all over the mall? My face is on every one of them. I'm practically famous! Heh-heh."

"Oh," Juni said. "That must be it."

"*But* as fascinating as I am, enough about me!" Webster said. When he laughed, his belly jiggled and wiggled over his pants. "We have to talk about the poor shoppers who are trapped in the virtual mall. They're being battered and bewildered. Sliced and diced! Figuratively speaking, of course."

"Hey," Juni said suspiciously. "That sounds familiar, too—"

"No time for small talk, Spy Boy," Webster interrupted. He clutched Juni's shoulders in his big, plump hands. "Think of all the people. You've got to find a way to help them!"

CHAPTER 6

Carmen looked at Webster. His brown eyes were practically bulging with concern. She walked over to the distraught man and placed a firm hand on his shoulder.

"Don't worry," she said. "I'm an expert hacker. I'll dismantle the villain's computer program in no time. And then you'll have your mall back, just the way it was before."

"Just . . . the way . . . it was . . . before," Webster said. His face slackened again, and his buggy eyes glazed over.

"I know," Juni said, putting his hand on Webster's other shoulder. "It will be a big relief."

"Oh, of course," Webster said. "I mean, where would we all be without all this beautiful, beautiful retail?"

"Oh . . . I don't know . . ." Dad said sarcastically. "Europe?"

"Gregorio," Mom chided him with a grin. Then

she turned to Webster. "Forgive my husband. You know non-Americans. They just don't understand the urge to shop till you drop."

"We better get started," Juni pointed out, "before the shoppers in the virtual mall start to take that phrase literally!"

"You're right," Webster said. His fleshy face became animated again and he pumped his fist in the air. "I'll help you. After all, I know the Mall of the Universe like the back of my hand. I'll show you the best places to look for this brilliant—I mean, uh, terrible—computer. Let's go!"

Waving the spies forward, Webster began to trot down the corridor. But Carmen held up her hand.

"Wait a minute," she said. "We're talking eight square miles of mall. Don't you think we should split up? We'll have that much more chance of actually succeeding."

"Ah, that's why my little girl's a Level One spy," Dad said, patting Carmen on the head. "Indeed, let's split up. You and Juni can head toward the amusement park in the mall's southern corner. Your mother and I will go with Webster in the opposite direction."

"Are you sure that's a good idea?" Webster asked, clasping and wringing his hands nervously.

"I mean, this bad guy. He could be big and strong. And dangerous!"

"Please," Juni said. "I know my computer geeks. Big and strong is not an issue."

"Hey!" Carmen growled defensively.

"Except where my sister is concerned, of course," Juni added, rolling his eyes. "Besides, Webster, you don't have to worry about us. We're highly trained spies. We know what we're doing."

"But . . ." Webster protested.

"Don't worry about it!" Carmen insisted. "We'll be fine. The day will be saved before you know it."

An hour later, Carmen and Juni were still tromping through the nonvirtual mall.

"Ugh," Carmen complained. "We're *never* gonna save the day at this rate!"

In their search for a seam into the virtual environment, she and Juni had been poking at store windows, peering into fountains, and swiping at the air with their fists. But they were turning up zilch.

Carmen sighed and kept walking. She found herself casting wistful glances in the direction of dormant clothes boutiques and sweet-smelling cosmetics shops. But after a few minutes of yearning, she tried to discard any daydreams about shopping. She had to focus on the mission!

Juni, on the other hand, seemed less concerned. When Carmen glanced his way, she saw that he'd drifted over to a hot-pretzel stand in the middle of the mall corridor.

"Juni," she admonished. "What are you doing?"

Juni circled the little pretzel cart, gazing at it curiously. It was a silver cube topped by a blue umbrella. To Carmen, it looked no different from the dozens of snack stands the Spy Kids had already passed.

"Look at that," Juni said, pointing to the silver cube. "It could be a seam. It's sort of shimmery. Maybe we should check it out."

"I know you, Juni," Carmen accused. "As usual, you're just stalling for a snack. And as usual, we don't have time for that! C'mon!"

She started to continue down the corridor. But Juni wouldn't budge.

"Juni!" Carmen barked in irritation.

Juni ignored her and began sifting through his shopping bag of gizmos. In a moment, he pulled out a little plastic squeeze-bottle.

"What is that?" Carmen said, trudging back to her brother irritably.

"An Uncle Machete special," Juni said. "It's called Peel Me An Onion."

"Huh?" Carmen blurted out in confusion.

Juni uncapped the bottle and squeezed it. A spurt of liquid shot out of the nozzle, splatting against the silver pretzel stand.

"Pee-ew!" Carmen cried as the liquid's fumes hit her square in the face. It smelled like the stinkiest onion in the world.

"Uncle Machete's glitches strike again," Juni said with a sniffle. Tears were spilling out of his eyes.

"No need to cry about it," Carmen said with a laugh.

"I am not crying!" Juni yelled. "It's just the onion fumes! If you tell anybody . . ."

But before Juni could come up with a good threat, he blinked through his tears in surprise. Something was happening to the pretzel stand!

Before the Spy Kids' eyes, the cube's silvery coating began to peel away. Beneath the silver was a layer of white fiberglass. Quickly, that peeled off, too, flopping onto the floor in a shimmery sheet. Next, a chunk of foam began to peel away.

"I get it!" Carmen cried. "That stinky stuff is peeling the pretzel stand in layers, just like an onion!"

"I wonder what layer's next!" Juni said breathlessly.

As he spoke, the foam layer fell to the floor, and the Spy Kids found themselves blinking at a shimmery, undulating hole.

"A seam!" Carmen and Juni cried together.

The portal was low to the ground and only a couple feet in diameter, but it was clearly an entryway into the alternate universe. Peeking through the hole, the Spy Kids could see a movie-theater marquee advertising nothing but boring, French films with subtitles. Nearby was a smoothie stand where the only ingredients were wheatgrass and beets.

"Talk about a horror show!" Juni breathed. "Looks like we're in the right place."

Giggling with glee, Carmen crouched down and began to clamber through the hole. But halfway through, she felt something like plastic wrap tighten across her head. As she tried to push through, the plastic grew more and more taut until it threw her backward like a slingshot!

"Hey!" she cried as she fell onto her backside, several feet from the seam. Indignantly, she clambered to her feet and tried leaping through the portal. She got a little farther this time, but once again, the invisible barrier pushed her back. Next, Juni shoved at Carmen's feet, but that didn't help, either.

"This is hopeless," Juni sputtered. "If only someone could pull us in from the other side . . ."

"How about Jake!" Carmen cried.

Juni gave Carmen a suspicious look. She'd find *any* excuse to get another glimpse of her crush. Teenagers!

Catching Juni's accusing glare, Carmen added defensively, "*And* Red and Mickey! They could help us."

Carmen quickly punched the cell phone number Jake had given her into her spy watch. After four rings, the mall rat answered breathlessly.

"Dude," he said to Carmen. "We just outran a survey taker."

"A survey taker?" Carmen asked.

"You know," Jake said. "Those chirpy people who corner you in the mall with clipboards and ask you annoying questions about shampoo and stuff."

"Yeah?"

"Well, in the virtual mall, they sort of hypnotize you," Jake said. "And before you know it, you're answering twenty thousand questions."

"Tell her how, right after we dodged the

clipboard mafia, I almost slid down the bottomless slide at the playground," Carmen heard Mickey say in the background. "Close call!"

"Clearly, we don't have any time to waste," Carmen said. "We found a seam, but we need some help. Can you come give us a yank?"

Carmen described her location. A few minutes later, Jake, Red, and Mickey arrived. They were all wearing oversized oven mitts.

"Cute, huh?" Red said, showing off her tomato-colored mitts. "I picked 'em up on the way over here. Hopefully, they'll cut down on the spark-age."

All three mall rats began to tug and pull on Juni's hands until he finally plunged through the seam with a pop. Next, they yanked Carmen through. She shot through the seam with such force that she landed in a heap—on Jake! Pulling off his now smoking oven mitt, Jake helped her to her feet.

"Hot stuff," he said with a grin.

"Thanks," Carmen replied, her face starting to turn red.

"Um, I meant the oven mitt," Jake said, dropping the glove to the floor and stomping out the little flame in its thumb.

"Oh," Carmen said. She was sure her face was as crimson as Red's pigtails.

"And, you're welcome," Jake said with a cock-eyed grin.

"Oh . . ." Carmen said again. But before she could get too swoony, Mickey cut in.

"Before you teenagers get all gushy," he said, rolling his eyes, "maybe you'll want to talk about something that really matters—like the computer hub for instance!"

CHAPTER 7

Carmen gasped and stared down at Mickey.

"You found the computer hub?" she demanded.

"Well, we *saw* it," Mickey said, sticking out his chin proudly. "Uh . . . maybe . . ."

Red stepped in front of Mickey and popped her strawberry gum loudly.

"Okay, enough showing off," she said. "Here's the scoop, see? We were running all over the mall when I saw a blue light glowing off in the distance. It was tucked into the fake palm trees in the Amazonian theme restaurant, the one with the real piranhas."

"Good eye," Juni said.

"Thanks!" Red said. "I never miss a Blue Light Special. So anyway, we were heading toward the light to check it out when *somebody* decided to stop and listen to some music. You know those guys with the crank-handled organs and the little monkeys that take your money?"

"I love those little monkeys!" Juni exclaimed.

"See!" Mickey said to Red with a pout. "It was an honest mistake."

"Uh-huh," Red said to him dryly.

Then she turned back to Carmen and Juni and continued. "So Mickey here decides to give the little monkey a quarter. And then the little monkey decides to morph into a giant gorilla! He chased us right out of the theme restaurant. Jake sacrificed his tiny TV for the cause."

"Yeah, I threw it at the gorilla," Jake said with a scowl. "Luckily, I thought to turn it on first. The big hairy ape got caught up in a Tarzan cartoon and we were able to dash."

Carmen smiled. Jake had serious spy potential!

"And that's when you called us and we came here," Red went on, bursting through Carmen's daydreams.

"Do you remember the coordinates of the blue light?" Juni asked briskly.

"Please, I know the layout of this mall better than I know my own house," Red said with a grin. "We'll get you there."

"Then let's go!" Juni cried. The five kids began racing through the mall. As they went, they passed lots of stunned shoppers. One—a straitlaced-looking man—seemed to have been forcibly dressed up in balloon sculptures. He tugged at the humiliating balloon duck resting on his head, but it wouldn't come off. Another shopper reeked of cheap perfume. And a frustrated woman was covered from head to toe with supersticky caramel corn.

"Don't worry," Juni yelled to them all. "Help is on the way."

"Thank goodness!" the sticky woman said. She clutched Juni's hand in gratitude as he ran by.

"No, thank *you*!" Juni said, glancing at the caramel corn that was now stuck to his palm. He was happily gnawing on the crunchy snack when suddenly a rumbling shook the floor. The spies and mall rats froze in front of a bookstore and glanced at each other nervously.

"Okay, what do you think that was?" Carmen asked.

"Maybe it was a bunch of happy shoppers, stampeding to a super sale at the department store around the corner?" Red suggested hopefully.

"Or skater kids, doing some triple ollies on the skate ramp downstairs?" Jake muttered pleadingly.

"Or maybe," Juni quavered, "it's our villain with another trick up his slee-EEEEEVE!"

No sooner had Juni made this conjecture than

the trick emerged—right out of the floor! The floorboards splintered, and through them rose a giant, sparkling boulder. It was made of a clear, glasslike substance and was cut into glinty planes and angles. The kids had to leap backward to avoid being splatted by the giant rock.

When the boulder finally shuddered to a halt, the kids scrambled to their feet and began running away from it.

Thhhhruump!

Another glinty rock erupted from the floor, cutting them off cold! They careened to the left.

Thruummmp!

And the right.

Thruuummp!

This time, when the boulder emerged, it popped out farther. The kids could see huge gold prongs, cradling the rock at its base.

"I recognize these things," Juni cried. "They're giant cubic zirconia rings."

"Cubic zir-WHAT?" Jake said, wiping shards of mall floor from his shoulders.

"Fake diamonds," Juni said. "You can buy them on the Web."

"Yeah, if you have really bad taste," Red cried. She dodged yet another zirconia as it burst through the floor. Then she spun around in a circle. Everywhere she looked, giant, fake diamonds stared back at her. The boulders had formed a perfect circle around the five kids.

"We're surrounded by cubic zirconia," Red blurted. "They've blocked us in!"

"Not for long," Carmen announced. She pulled a few sticks of gum from her mesh shopping bag and handed one to Red.

"No, thanks," Red said, opening her mouth to show Carmen her wad of bright, strawberry gum. "I've already got some."

"This isn't for blowing bubbles," Carmen said. "It's Sticky-Sole Gum. It's not the fanciest gadget the OSS has ever come up with, but it's a classic. Chew it up and stick it to the bottoms of your shoes. Then wait three seconds and start climbing!

"And besides," Carmen added as she ripped the wrapper off her own stick of gum. "It's red! Cinnamon-flavored. You'll like it!"

Grinning, Red spat out her strawberry wad and popped the Sticky-Sole Gum into her mouth. Carmen tossed sticks to Mickey, Jake, and Juni. Mere seconds later, the kids shoes were gummed up. They were able to climb over the cubic zirconia easily. They were free!

No sooner had they landed outside the glittery prison than another thumping began to fill the mall.

"What now?" Carmen cried.

"I think we're trapped in a giant, tacky infomercial," Red shrieked. With a trembling finger, she pointed down the corridor.

Juni followed Red's gaze. Five tall, stiff people were making their way toward them. And for some reason, instead of running, they were hopping! Each hop covered about ten feet. They were gaining on the kids quickly.

As the intruders got closer, Juni blinked in disbelief.

They weren't people! They were eight-foot-tall dolls! One was wearing a green, satin dress with a hoopskirt. Another had blond braids and a stiff, white Dutch cap. Yet another wore deep purple, Victorian velvet. They all had porcelain faces plastered with blank, rosy smiles. Their feet were moored to giant, plastic pedestals.

"They're massive collector's dolls!" Red announced. "And they're gonna stomp us!"

"Run!" Carmen ordered!

Thwuck, thwuck, thwuck, thwuck.

The kids' Sticky-Soles made puckery, sucking

noises as they scattered. Carmen and Red darted into the bookstore. Juni and Jake ducked behind the crags of one of the giant, cubic zirconia.

But Mickey stood his ground. He was going to take on the quickly approaching collector's dolls!

"Mickey!" Carmen screamed at him. "Get out of there! Now!"

"I would if I could!" Mickey shouted back. "But I'm stuck!"

The other kids gasped. Mickey wasn't trying to be a hero! His little legs were simply no match for the Sticky-Soles!

But perhaps the Spy Kids' gadgets were! Juni stepped out from behind his cubic zirconium and raised his wrist to eye level. He pressed a few buttons on his spy watch. Suddenly, a bright red laser beam shot out of the watch. Juni aimed the beam at Mickey. As the red stream of light traveled along the floor toward the boy, it left a smoking black trail.

"Hey, watch it with that thing!" Mickey shrieked.

"Believe me, I am!" Juni called back. Carefully, he moved the laser beam onto Mickey's shoes. In two seconds, Mickey's shoelaces had disappeared in a plume of smoke. Grinning, Mickey hopped out of his shoes and got ready to run for cover.

And that's *just* when the huge, plastic hand of one of the collector's dolls—the one with the corkscrew curls and white sailor dress—scooped him up! She began hopping away, with Mickey tucked under her plastic arm.

"Spy Kids," Mickey screamed. "Help meeeeeee!"

"**M**ickey!" Jake cried, running out from behind his hiding spot by the cubic zirconia. He stood out in the open, gasping with fear. "We have to do something—I gotta save my little bro!"

"Well, you can't save him if you get caught yourself," Carmen cried. Over Jake's shoulder, she spotted another collector's doll. It was the monstrous Dutch girl, and she was advancing upon Jake, fast! Carmen dove at Jake, shoving him out of the doll's grip just in time. Together, they rolled to the side of the corridor and skittered beneath a bench. For the time being, they were out of harm's way.

Meanwhile, Red and Juni had climbed to the top of the furthest cubic zirconia, well out of reach of the cumbersome dolls. From a safe distance the two boys surveyed the area. Red was staring in horror at the large Shirley Temple doll, who was making off with Mickey.

"We'll save you, Mickey!" she called. But when she turned to Juni, her eyes were brimming with fearful tears.

"We *will* save him," Juni said to Red. "Don't worry. Wait here where it's safe."

Quickly, Juni pulled a sucker dart out of his utility belt and aimed it directly at Carmen and Jake's bench.

Splat!

The sucker dart—which had a skinny, but strong, cable attached to its back end—made a direct hit on the bench. Juni anchored his end of the cable on one of the fake diamond ring's gold prongs. Then he swiftly and confidently walked the tightrope down to Carmen and Jake. Sliding beneath the bench to join them, Juni quickly retracted his cable back into the dart gun with a *whiizzzz.*

"Ready for a rescue?" he asked Carmen.

"Ready!" Carmen said grimly, and a little breathlessly.

"Me, too!" Jake declared. When Carmen and Juni glanced at him skeptically, he blurted out, "What? You expect me to just sit here while some doll runs off with my bro? No! He's my brother. I'm helping!"

Carmen glanced at *her* little brother. She had to admit, she knew just how Jake was feeling. So, she nodded brusquely and said, "Okay, but you have to do everything we tell you."

"Roger," Jake said. "Anything for Mickey. Man, those dolls are really whack!"

"Hey," Juni said. His green eyes gleamed. "That's it! Whack-A-Mole!"

"Otherwise known as Spy Maneuver Number Thirty-Six-C?" Carmen asked. She got a similar gleam in her brown eyes.

"Precisely," Juni said. "Perfect plan for three people."

"Are you talking about that arcade game where you thunk the moles on the head when they pop out of their holes?" Jake sputtered. "Dudes, that's a cool game and all, but there's no way we're going to be able to just conk out those dolls! They're huge."

"No, Jake," Juni said. "*They're* not the moles. *We* are!"

"What?" Jake squeaked. But there was no time for any more chatting. The Spy Kids got busy peeling the Sticky-Soles off their shoes and replacing them with sets of remote-control Pop Springs. Carmen pulled a third set of the springs out of her bag and helped Jake strap them onto his own shoes.

"Good thing I packed Mom's Pop Springs in my bag," Carmen said. "I think that they'll just about fit you."

"But what do I do with these things?" Jake asked. He stared down at the flattened springs on the soles of his feet.

"Just follow our lead," Carmen said with a daring smile. Then she glanced at both boys and barked, "Let's move!"

The three kids began tiptoeing across the floor toward Mickey and his curly-topped captor. Just as the Spy Kids had expected, the other dolls spotted them right away.

Clomp! Clomp! Clomp!

They were coming over!

"Wait . . . wait . . ." Carmen cautioned her partners. The Victorian doll was the closest. She was bearing down on Juni.

"*Now!*" Carmen shouted.

Juni hit the button on his Pop Springs' remote control. The springs sproinged out of his soles, popping Juni into the air. He flew up, up, up, whizzing right by the doll's porcelain nose. Her glassy blue eyes blinked in surprise.

She whacked at him—and missed.

"Jake!" Carmen cried to the stunned mall rat. "Now you!"

Though he still looked flummoxed, Jake nodded and hit the small red button on his own remote control.

Sproiiinng!

As Jake flew into the air, the doll whacked at *him*. She missed again!

The doll spun to get a crack at Carmen. And this time, she almost connected! As Carmen felt the doll's plastic fist whiz by her ear, she did a perfect midair toe touch. She dodged out of the doll's way just in time.

"Careful, Carmen!" Jake cried out. His voice was filled with concern.

Carmen couldn't believe she could blush in the middle of Spy Maneuver #36-C, but that's exactly what she did.

And despite all the blushing, Spy Maneuver #36-C was working! After all that fruitless whacking, the Victorian doll was looking a little befuddled.

She began to teeter.

And then she tottered.

Juni gave her leg a shove and she toppled over

altogether! When she crashed to the floor, her big arms popped off her body and her plastic pedestal rolled away.

"These collector's dolls are cheap!" Carmen said in disgust.

"They're also out for revenge!" Juni said, pointing over Carmen's shoulder. Sure enough, the remaining four dolls, including the one clutching the howling Mickey, were hopping over to them now.

"Perfect!" Carmen cried.

"Perfect?!" Jake blustered. "Dude, we're gonna get flattened."

"No, we won't," Carmen said. "Just . . ."

"I know," Jake interrupted. "Follow your lead. You don't have to convince me."

Flushing with pride, Carmen lined up between Juni and Jake. She poised her finger over her Pop Springs remote-control button. And then she waited.

Thump! Thump! Thump!

Carmen did a quick calculation in her head. The dolls would be close enough in approximately 2.5 seconds.

"Ready . . ." she said to the boys. "Set . . . *Sproing!*"

Sproing! Sproing! Sproing!

Juni popped to the left, just before the hoop-skirted doll squashed him with her shiny black shoes. Jake popped right, barely missing the Dutch doll's razor-sharp cap.

But Carmen shot forward—directly into Shirley Temple's gut.

Pop!

That was the sound of Mickey, popping out of the doll's plastic grip!

Plop!

And that was Mickey, landing right on top of his brother Jake. The two boys sprawled on the floor in a momentary daze. Then they started cackling triumphantly and pumping the air with their fists. They gave each other a quick, happy hug.

Thump! Thump! Thump!

"There's no time for a reunion now," Juni yelled at the mall rats. "Jake, you and Mickey go get Red and hide. We'll finish off these dolls and call you when the coast is clear."

"Thanks, dudes!" Jake yelled. He grabbed Mickey by the elbow and hit his remote-control button one more time. Together, the brothers popped up and out of danger.

Thump! Thump! Thump!

After watching Jake and Mickey make their escape, Juni turned his attention back to the looming dolls. Two were coming at the Spy Kids from the front. And two were behind them. The dolls were moving fast.

Without taking his eyes off the advancing monster dolls, Juni whispered to his sister, "Okay, this should be a cinch. I'll take the Dutch girl and the Victorian. You take the other two. Okay, Carmen? Carmen?!"

Juni glanced to his left. Then he looked to his right. Where had Carmen gone?

Fearfully, Juni looked up. Sure enough, Carmen was in the grip of the hoopskirted doll! Her mouth was gagged with the doll's pretty green hair bow, and her hands were tied.

Sproing!

Without thinking twice, Juni used his Pop Springs to jump onto the doll's voluminous skirt. He clutched the slippery fabric as he began climbing up toward his sister.

"Don't worry, Carmen," Juni called up to his stolen sib. "I'll get you out of this."

"Mmmmmm!" Carmen grunted behind her silken gag. To Juni's ears, her muffled cry sounded like "What?"

"I *said* I'll get you out of this!" Juni said, climbing a few more steps and grabbing the doll's silk sash.

"Mmmm! Mmm-mmm-mmmph!" Carmen said. Her eyes were bulging as she stared over Juni's shoulder.

"What?" Juni said. He glanced behind him just in time to see a giant, plastic hand grab at his shirt collar. Effortlessly, the Dutch doll plucked Juni from her comrade's hoopskirt. She dangled Juni high above the ground.

The Spy Kids were captured!

CHAPTER 9

"**H**ey, easy!" Juni protested as the Dutch doll tossed him like, well, a rag doll onto the floor of a huge, high-ceilinged atrium in the center of the mall. A moment later, Carmen's doll dumped her in as well. She collided with Juni, and they both tumbled to the floor.

Whooooosh!

Black bars suddenly rose out of the floor, sur-rounding the Spy Kids on all sides. They were now in a cage that reached all the way to the towering atrium ceiling! Some of the bars were six inches wide. Others were a foot thick. Still others were only an inch across.

"How completely random!" Juni said. He jumped to his feet and spun around to assess the uneven bars. On the other side of the bars, the col-lector's dolls began to quickly hop away, leaving Carmen and Juni alone in their cage.

"You won't get away with this," Juni called after

the dolls. He ran up to the bars and grabbed two of them.

Zzoootttzz!

"Ow!" Juni shouted, leaping backward. Angry red welts rose up on his palms. "Of course! The bars are virtual *and* electrified. What next?"

"Mmmmmm!" Carmen replied. Her mouth was still gagged with the doll's satiny green ribbon.

"I can't understand you," Juni scowled.

"Mmmmm!" Carmen screeched.

"Okay, okay," Juni said, stumbling over to Carmen. "But if I ungag you, you have to promise not to yell at me anymore."

"Wammm-emem," Carmen said.

"That sounded awfully like 'Whatever,' to me, but I'll untie you anyway," Juni said. He crouched behind his sister and nimbly unknotted the ropes around her hands. Groaning with relief, Carmen untied her own gag. Massaging her jaw, she got to her feet and stared at the bars.

"Hey," she said suddenly, pointing to the base of the bars. "There are numbers at the bottom of this cage."

Then she slapped her forehead.

"I know what this is!" she cried. "Instead of bars, our prison is made of bar *codes*! You know, those stripy symbols on every consumer product?"

"Now, do you believe me when I say that shopping stinks?" Juni said with an exasperated sigh. Then he pressed a button on his spy watch.

"Let's check in with Mom and Dad," he said. "Hopefully they've found a seam and can come rescue—"

Before Juni had a chance to finish his sentence—much less call their parents on his spy watch—a cheerful-looking couple stepped out from behind a 'You Are Here' kiosk and walked up to the bars. The woman wore a cardigan sweater and a navy blue headband in her shiny blond hair. The man wore a red tie and a twinkly smile.

"Hi there, young fella!" the man said.

"They must be shoppers," Carmen whispered to Juni. "Although they don't seem very traumatized to be trapped in the virtual mall."

"I don't care *who* they are, as long as they help us," Juni whispered. "They look friendly enough. Maybe they'll help us break free of this virtual chicken coop."

Then he turned to the couple.

"Hi there, yourself," Juni said jovially. "Perhaps you could give us a hand. . . ."

"You betcha," the blond woman chirped in a

twangy North Dakota accent. "I'm Candy, and this here is Andy. We'd be happy to help ya out. But first, can we ask y'all just a few questions. . . ?"

Candy and Andy each pulled a clipboard from behind their backs. Attached to each clipboard, with a silvery chain, was a pencil.

"Let's start with your name, age, and approximately what time of day you were born," Candy began.

"And then we'll move on to the dates upon which you lost each of your baby teeth," Andy said, licking the lead of his pencil, "followed by family pet history."

Carmen's horror mounted as she saw how many pages were wedged onto the clipboards.

"Survey takers!" she hissed to Juni. "Jake told me about them. They hypnotize you, and you're stuck answering their silly consumer questions for an eternity!"

"That's terrible," Juni said, blinking widely at Carmen. "But could you hold that thought?"

Then he turned to the chirpy Candy. "Now, let's see," he said, "I lost my upper-right bicuspid in the spring of my sixth year. Ah, I can still remember what the tooth fairy brought me. A yo-yo and a dollar."

"Uh-huh," Candy said eagerly. "And tell me,

Carmen, what kind of shampoo do you use?"

"I refuse to answer your inane questions," Carmen said, sticking out her chin. "But if you must know, I use peach-melba shampoo for curly hair, and then I sometimes finish with a nice straw-berry-cream rinse. . . ."

Juni's mouth was dry.

His eyelids were heavy.

His head was pounding. He didn't know how long he and Carmen had been here, sprawled on the floor of the bar code jail, answering the survey takers' questions. But it seemed like a long, long time.

"Uh-huh, super," the apple-cheeked Andy was saying. He flipped over yet another page on his clipboard. "And when you brush your teeth, would you say you make up-and-down motions, or side to side?"

"Ummm," Juni groaned, trying to picture him-self in his bathroom at home, brushing his teeth. Ah . . . home . . . where there were no price tags . . . no 'You Are Here' kiosks . . . no indoor fountains and soaring, glass-topped atria. . . .

Juni's eyelids were even heavier now. They were just about to fall shut when something glimmered in his eye. He perked up a bit. What was that?

The sparkle happened again. Something was flashing from the glass people mover, which was halted on its monorail far above the atrium. Juni glanced at Carmen to see if she could see it. But she was immersed in telling the survey takers about the way she tied her shoes.

Juni blinked rapidly and stared up at the flashes again. When his eyes came into focus, he realized he was gazing up at Red, Jake, and Mickey! They were peering down into Carmen and Juni's jail cell from the people mover's window. Red was bobbling one of her ruby rhinestone barrettes. It reflected the sunshine streaming through the atrium's glass ceiling. Those were the flashes that had caught Juni's eye. In fact, the flashes seemed to have a rhythm. . . .

Suddenly, Juni gasped. The sparkles *did* have a rhythm. And a rhyme and a reason! They were Morse code! Quickly, Juni translated Red's flashes into two words: UPC number.

Huh?

Confused, Juni nudged Carmen. In her survey-taking daze, she ignored him. Juni nudged her harder. Finally, he elbowed her in the ribs.

"Ow!" Carmen blurted, glaring over at her

brother. He looked at her pointedly, then glanced up at the people mover. She followed his gaze and gasped when she saw Jake, Mickey, and Red, flashing her barrettes.

While Juni took over the survey answers, Carmen deciphered the Morse code. The moment she got to the "r" in "UPC number," she gasped in recognition!

Of course, she thought. Why didn't I think of that? To ring up an item on a cash register, you either scan in its bar code or type in the UPC number at the bottom of the bars. It's like a bar-code safecracker.

Carmen looked hungrily at the numbers lining the bottom of the giant bar code before her. Then she shook the last bit of survey-induced bleariness from her head and began surreptitiously typing into her spy watch.

"Golly, good answer, Juni," Andy was saying. "Now let's talk about potatoes. Do you prefer them baked, mashed, fried, scalloped . . . ?"

Carmen lifted the tiny antenna of her spy watch's wireless modem. Then she began feverishly—if quietly—hacking into the national UPC network. A few deft keystrokes later and she was in!

Hoping she had gotten everything correct, she

braced her feet and typed in the giant bar code's UPC number.

Fwoooom!

The uneven stripes of the bar code whooshed back into the floor. Carmen and Juni stood still for a moment as they looked at where the bars had been. Then they grinned. The Spy Kids were free!

"Juni," Carmen cried. "Run!"

Now that the bar codes had disappeared, Carmen and Juni just had to deal with Candy and Andy. The survey takers were looking far less cheery now that their captive audience was not so captive.

"You can't leave now," Candy growled. "If you don't complete the survey, the whole thing is null and void."

"Void this!" Carmen yelled. She grabbed Candy's clipboard and thwacked the survey taker over the head with it. While Candy staggered away, Carmen darted across the atrium.

Meanwhile, Juni took Andy's clipboard and yanked the pencil free. He looped its silver chain around Andy's wrists and knotted it tight. Then he dashed after Carmen.

When he caught up to her, Carmen was just emerging from a nearby toy store with two extra-large pogo sticks. She tossed one to Juni.

"I just tried one of these and bonked my head on the ceiling," Carmen told him. "I think the virtual environment supersized them."

"Just what we need!" Juni crowed. The Spy Kids climbed onto the pogo sticks and positioned themselves beneath the glass people mover. They both jumped at the same time. One mighty bounce sent them soaring high into the air.

Splat! Splat!

"Ohm-kay," Juni said. With his face smashed up against the glass of the people mover, it was a little hard to talk. "I guess we miscalculated the distance, a bit."

Carmen unstuck her own face from the glass and shook her head woozily. Like Juni, she was clinging to the people mover's door with her fingertips.

"Hey, at least we made it up here," she sighed. Jake poked his head through the window and gave the Spy Kids a smile.

"Another awesome splat from the Spy Kids," he said. "Have you guys ever thought about going into video game design?"

"Hardy-har," Juni said dryly. "Now is not the time. Wanna give us a hand?"

Within a few minutes, Carmen had hacked into

the people mover's computer-driven engine and steered the car down the monorail to the Amazonian theme restaurant. Red pointed to a faint blue glow between the fake alligator pool and the fake volcano.

"See?" she said with satisfaction. "Just like I told you—Blue Light Special."

"Well," Carmen said, "when in the jungle . . ."

She reached into her shopping bag and pulled out five green ropes with silver rings on their ends. She handed them out.

"They're not exactly vines," she grinned, "but they'll get us down!"

The kids clamped the ropes onto the people mover's exterior and rappelled down into the depths of the fake jungle. They landed right in front of a large, metal cube. It was fronted by a small door that was full of large bolts and locks. The door was humming and pulsing with so much energy, it was giving off a blue glow. A glow so bright that Red had seen it from across the mall.

"This has got to be it! On the other side of that door we'll find the computer hub and, I'm sure, our mystery villain," Carmen cried. "We have to let our parents know before we storm in. Who knows what sort of defense this madman has waiting for us. We might need backup."

Nodding in agreement, Juni pressed the walkie-talkie button on his spy watch.

"Mom, Dad," he said proudly. "We've located the computer hub. Repeat, we're at the hub. What's your location? Over."

Then Juni cocked his head and waited for his parents' response.

"Sorry, Spy Kids, your mom and dad are indisposed," said an oily-smooth voice. "And as for their whereabouts, only I know!"

"Webster?" Juni questioned into his spy watch. "Is that you?"

"Indeedy, do!" Webster said. "And have I got a surprise for you. It's just around that fake boulder about ten feet to your left."

Carmen and Juni glanced to their left. There was a boulder just where Webster had said it would be. The siblings glanced at each other in surprise. They knew at once that Webster was watching them.

"He must have us on a surveillance camera," Carmen whispered to her brother. "After all, he is head of security."

With a shrug, the Spy Kids headed toward the boulder.

"You better stay here while we check this out," Carmen told the mall rats over her shoulder. "Stay behind that shrub."

When they rounded the big foam rock, the Spy Kids saw a big bank of computer monitors, mounted into the fake volcano's wall. Each screen was identically filled with pulsing stars and a window that flashed, CLICK HERE!

Juni looked around wildly.

"Click with what?" he blurted.

Whizzzzz.

As if in response to his question, a panel suddenly opened beneath one of the screens and a mouse and mouse pad whooshed out of the wall. Juni grabbed the mouse and double-clicked on the window. Suddenly, the computer screens sprang to life. The Spy Kids found themselves blinking at a pulsating, cartoony soundstage festooned with lamps, jewelry, toys, clothes, dolls, and other merchandise. Big, yellow price tags were attached to each item.

And dancing in front of these wares was Webster. But just like the toys and jewelry, the schlubby security guard was shiny and new. His frizzy brown curls had been replaced by a shellacked, blond hairstyle. His paunch was flattened, and his shoulders were broadened. His chin was strong and clefted, and his teeth were sparkling white.

"A new wallet for your dough, a new car in which to go," Webster said, thrusting his grinning face into the camera, "computers in the know, mowers with which to mow! Buy them all for prices loooow, on Whoppershopper.com."

Juni gasped.

"Webster Pichman! Of course," he sputtered. "How could I have missed that. He's Web D.C. Pichman. Dot Com is his middle name! He's the mastermind behind Whoppershopper.com. I *knew* he looked familiar!"

"Whoppershopper.com," Carmen blurted. "Is that the Web site with those ridiculous skater outfits?"

"Yeah," Juni said morosely. "Not to mention the video games and toys and . . . cubic zirconia rings. And . . ."

"Let me guess," Carmen said softly, her heart sinking. "Tacky collector's dolls?"

"You got it, kiddos," Webster said, flashing another sparkly grin at the camera. He leaned in closer to the screen. "And that's not all! If you buy now, I will throw in my Blue Light Special. For a very special, one-time-only price, you can get your-selves not one, but two . . . meddling *parents*!"

Suddenly, the camera swung away from Web. It skimmed over a gigantic mainframe computer, loaded with bells and whistles. The bells were ring-ing. The whistles were whistling.

And the camera kept moving. Finally, it came to rest on—Mom and Dad! They were bound, gagged, and gazing at the camera in absolute terror!

"**I** can't believe it," Carmen sputtered to the computer screens. The camera had swung away from the captive Cortezes and refocused on Webster. "*You're* the villain?"

"What, you're surprised?" Webster said, carefully smoothing his hand over his shiny helmet of oiled hair. "Some spies. That I thought you would have surmised."

"Cut the bad Dr. Seuss routine and tell us what you're after, Pichman," Juni raged.

"It's simple dollars and cents," Web said, rubbing his now manicured fingertips together. "Without the Mall of the Universe to feed shoppers' greed, where are they left to turn? Whoppershopper.com! They've already started buying, buying, buying. And I couldn't let you silly spies muck up my profit margin by reopening this mall, could I?"

Juni glared. "You'll never—"

"—get away with it?" Web said, rolling his eyes. "Who's spouting clichés now, kiddies? I've got your parents, locked away tight. Mess with my computer, and they'll feel my might."

"You said we could have our parents back for a price," Juni said to Web. "What sort of price are you talking about?"

"Please . . . I don't need your cash," Web said, examining his sparkly teeth in a tacky, faux silver hand mirror. "All I want is for you to dash. Leave the Mall of the Universe be, and I'll let your parents go free."

Juni didn't want this villain to see him sweat—or panic. So, he continued to glare at the computers, his chin thrust out defiantly. But out of the camera's range, he surreptitiously reached for his spy watch. He quickly typed in an instant message to Carmen.

"What do we do?" he typed without looking at his watch. "This guy's rotten rhyming is giving me a headache. What's more, if we try to dismantle his computer program, he's going to do something horrible to Mom and Dad!"

Juni hit SEND. Carmen's spy watch buzzed and she glanced down and read Juni's IM. Another moment later, Juni received her reply.

"Not if I can help it," she'd written. "Keep him talking."

Juni turned back to the computer.

Keep him talking?! he said to himself. What can I possibly have to talk about with a greedy archvillain who's kidnapped my parents? The only things that leaped to his mind were angry insults. So, Juni shrugged and let them fly.

"Listen, Web," he sneered. "I don't know why you're even bothering. Your skater clothes are completely uncool. And cubic zirconia and collector's dolls? Please! Those things are tackier than wet paint. People are going to get sick of Whoppershopper.com and move on to something else faster than you can say, 'Down, down, download.'"

Web's blue eyes narrowed and his jutting jaw clenched. It had worked. Juni had honed in on Web's worst fear.

"That's what you think!" Web hissed at the Spy Kid. "Sure, my goods are pure junk. I know that. But that doesn't matter. My genius is in the sales technique. Nobody, but *nobody*, can resist the pitch of Web D.C. Pichman!"

With that, Web snapped his fingers. A surge of cheesy elevator music poured out of the computer monitors. A pretty woman in a blue satin dress danced into the camera's range and twirled around in a circle. She smiled directly into the camera. She was wearing a pair of glittery, blue earrings beneath her supersprayed blond hairdo.

"Allow my lovely assistant to show you our genuine, three-carat, almost-not-artificial sapphire earrings," Web began as the woman continued to mug for the camera. "Nothing sets blue eyes afire like the spark of sapphire. You'll be so sure they're real, this price will seem like a steal. . . ."

As Web thrust a matching glittery bracelet and necklace at the camera and prattled on about low, low prices, Carmen furtively dialed Jake's cell-phone number into her spy watch. Then she sent *him* an instant message. In fact, she sent him a series of them. In the first, she told him all about their dot-com bad guy. Then she began sending explicit instructions for breaking into the computer hub door.

Instantly, there was a message from Jake.

"No prob," he wrote. "I've got Red listening to the door for clicks while I spin the combination lock. And Mickey's working the little bolts, 'cuz his fingers are so small. Just keep the instructions coming and we'll break into this computer hub faster than you can say Going-Out-of-Business-Super-Software-Sale."

Carmen kept typing.

And Pichman kept pitching.

And Juni kept egging him on.

"But *how* do you get your nonstick pans so non-sticky?" he asked Web challengingly.

"My boy, let me tell you!" Web gushed. He patted his slick hair before continuing on. "Our patented pan is a peerless performer. It's the protective coating of powdered pewter that makes the magic happen. . . ."

As the supervillain worked himself into a super-selling tizzy, Carmen got a final IM from Jake.

"Dude! We're totally in!" the message read.

Carmen nudged Juni with her elbow. Slowly and silently, the Spy Kids sneaked away from the bank of computer monitors. As they slipped back around the boulder on their way to the computer hub, Carmen peeked over her shoulder. Just as she'd hoped, Pichman was so wrapped up in his sleazy sales pitch, he hadn't even noticed that his audience was MIA!

Carmen and Juni hurried over to the mall rats. Red and Mickey were doing a triumphant dance of joy outside the computer hub door, which was standing ajar. Jake, ever the "kewl" one, merely leaned against a fake tree, his ankles crossed casually. But a gleeful grin was plastered on his face. He caught Carmen's eye and winked.

As Carmen and Juni ran up to the mall rats, Red quit dancing. They all knew that it was time to get down to business. Carmen pointed at the hub's thick steel door and curled her lip.

"Inside that room is Web D.C. Pichman, a villain who spits on everything we stand for," she seethed. "Like peaceful shopping. And food-court hanging. The whole magical microcosm that we know, and love, as the mall."

"Yeah," Mickey said, pumping one of his little fists in the air. "I want to see this baddie go down! Bring back our mall!"

Jake set his jaw and agreed, "Tscha. Let's get in there and slap the cuffs on that sleazy dude."

Jake was *so* spy material. And it was a lucky thing! To rescue two spy parents, dismantle the virtual-reality program cloaking the mall, *and* arrest Web, Carmen and Juni were definitely going to need some backup.

"Okay," she whispered to the mall rats. "Stay close to me and Juni. And if anything gets hairy, remember the golden rule of spying."

"What's that?" Mickey breathed.

"When in doubt," Juni informed him sagely, "fake it. And when faking fails, duck!"

"Wise words, dude," Jake said. "Let's go!"

The five kids lined up. Then Carmen gritted her teeth and kicked the unlocked computer hub door wide open. She and Juni jumped through the door first, their dukes raised and their voices sharp.

"Freeze, Web!" Juni barked.

"The jig is up," Carmen added.

But when the kids paused to scope out the computer hub, their voices evaporated into surprised squeaks. Then gasps of shock!

The Spy Kids gaped at what they saw. Because what they saw was precisely—nothing! They were standing in a completely empty, gunmetal-gray room. Where was the humming mainframe? Where was the garish display of tacky goods?! Web Pichman was nowhere to be seen, and the Cortez parents were AWOL, too. The room was as blank as a dead computer screen.

In fact, the very room in which the kids were standing seemed to be fading away. First, the walls became wavy and watery. Then, they slowly became transparent. Finally, with a burst of static and a flurry of shimmery dots, the walls evaporated entirely!

The dumbfounded crew of kids found themselves standing in the fake Amazonian jungle.

Juni's face fell.

"This was just an illusion!" he said. "Another part of Web's evil, virtual environment."

Suddenly, Web Pichman's silky-smooth voice erupted from the loudspeakers planted all over the mall.

"How'd you like that Blue Light Special, kiddos?" he boomed with a sinister cackle. "A real deal, eh?"

"Hey, bad guy! Nice ruse," Mickey said to the air. "But come fight us in person and we'll see who's got the fuse!"

"Uh, leave the rhyming to the experts, kid," Web said through the speakers.

"Why *don't* you come face us in person?" Juni demanded. "Or are you *scared* of us spies?"

"Pshaw!" Web bellowed. "Meet me in the food court in ten."

"We're there," Carmen said.

With that, the Spy Kids ran out of the theme restaurant with their buds in tow. They began dashing through the mall.

"Hurry," Carmen huffed as they ran past the indoor horse racing track and dodged the mist of the MOTU waterfalls. "The food court is about a mile away. If we run, we'll just make it."

The kids shot past the faux Florida alligator farm and the giant cotton candy machine. But when they approached the video arcade, Red called out, "Wait! There's a back door in this arcade. We can take a shortcut through it. I've done it dozens of times. It'll cut our trip in half."

"We need every minute we can get," Carmen said. "I want to beat Web to the food court. Maybe we'll have time to set a trap for him. Lead the way, Red."

"Man," Red said, grinning through a new wad of cherry gum. "Spying's almost as much fun as shopping! C'mon!"

The kids ran into the arcade. And then, the kids ground to a halt. They'd expected a familiar game room—black rubber floors, crowded, flashing video games, and a dusky, dimly lit atmosphere.

"I keep forgetting," Jake said in an awestruck voice. "We're not in our good ol' MOTU anymore. This joint's been virtualized."

In spades! The floors had transformed into a bubbly, floaty substance that felt like a cross between water and Jell-O. The video games had become huge, three-dimensional—and predatory!

"Whoa!" Juni yelled, jumping out of the way just as a medieval sword whistled out of one game. "That was a close one—"

RrrrrRRRRRRR!

"Agh!" Juni cried. This time, a fat race-car tire had whooshed out of another video game, nearly

99

flattening Juni before whizzing back into the game.

"Okay," Red said nervously. "The shortcut was obviously not the best idea. But the alternate door is just through this back room. Should we make a run for it?"

"Ah!" Carmen cried, ducking to dodge a leaping, animated frog. But then she nodded. "We've come this far. And here's motivation for running. There's a bunch of retro Ms. Pac-Mans heading straight for us!"

The kids began to race through the arcade as a small army of bigmouthed yellow dots skimmed after them, chomping hungrily at their heels. They'd almost made it to the door when Mickey tripped! The other kids heard him fall to the floor with a grunt. When they spun around, they saw Mickey cowering under the hot breath of a virtual dragon! It must have popped out of a nearby video game the moment Mickey hit the dirt.

"Mickey!" Carmen yelled. She started to run toward the little boy. But Jake grabbed her by the shoulders.

"You don't have time to hang around here," he told her. "You and Juni have got to get to the food court!"

"But we can't leave when Mickey's in trouble," Carmen gasped. She was reaching for her utility belt, trying to size up the best gadget for fighting dragons.

"Believe me, Carmen," Jake said. "That dragon is the star of King Arthur's Gore. It's my fave video game! I've held the high score for the past two years! I can totally take him."

To prove it, Jake leaped over to the dragon. As he went, he scooped up an armful of virtual rocks that were piled on the arcade floor. He began winging the rocks at the beast with expert aim. This gave Mickey a chance to scurry out of the creature's reach. But Jake kept fighting. Every time the irritated dragon spewed a breath of fire, he calmly and nimbly jumped out of the way. When the dragon lunged at him, he hit it with a virtual rock. Meanwhile, Red and Mickey hovered safely by the arcade's back door.

"Go on!" Jake said to the Spy Kids over his shoulder. "I've got this covered. The dragon's only playing at level two, for Pete's sake. I'll have him slain in five minutes. Then we'll come find you."

"Are you sure?" Carmen cried.

"Yes!" Jake said, easily sidestepping the dragon's

barbed tail as it took a swing at him. "Good luck with Web!"

Carmen flashed Jake a thank-you smile. Then she and Juni darted through the back door and looked around. Red was right! The food court was only a few yards away.

Carmen gave Juni a sidelong glance. She didn't dare speak out loud, in case Web was lurking nearby, listening. So she merely pointed at the Swat 'n' Splat hanging from her utility belt. He nodded in approval. The Swat 'n' Splat was one of their Uncle Machete's most effective—and messy—criminal-catching gizmos. Deploying it unleashed a giant flyswatter that squashed a villain flat and kept him still long enough for the Spy Kids to cuff him. Both Carmen and Juni knew it would be the perfect gizmo to take Web Pichman down.

As they crept stealthily into the food court, Carmen's and Juni's every spy sense was at high alert. Carmen took in the giant, fiberglass cheeseburger in the center of the food court and wondered if Web might be hiding behind it. She lifted her spy watch and pressed the heat sensor button. If there was a warm body behind that burger, her spy watch would tell her.

But the scan turned up cold.

Meanwhile, Juni eyed the virtual restaurants suspiciously. He didn't see Web in Wokky Talk—where the Chinese vegetables screamed in protest as they were stir-fried. Nor was the villain lurking in the Yo-Yo Fro-Yo shop, where the sweet frozen yogurt always melted before a frustrated snacker could take a bite.

"That Web is a sick man," Juni muttered, shuddering at the snack abuse. "Tell you what, Carmen. Why don't you search over by the Hot Dog Hoedown and I'll check out the Pickle Picker. . . . Carmen?"

Juni suddenly realized he'd been talking to thin air. His sister had disappeared!

"Carmen!" he cried, spinning around in search of his spy partner.

Zzzzzzzz!

Juni followed the zipping sound. There was Carmen—in the grip of a giant, mechanical arm! It had plunged out of the kitchen of a nearby cinnamon roll shop! Carmen was writhing and struggling against the mechanical arm's claw, but the giant silver prongs held her tight.

"Run, Juni!" she cried. "Don't get caught—"

"Aaaaaah!" Juni screamed. No sooner had Carmen's warning echoed across the food court than he felt the grip of another giant claw around his own middle.

"Carrrrrmeeeennn!" Juni screeched as the arm lifted him off the ground and whipped him backward. Juni twisted and turned so hard, he could feel his red curls flopping against his face. But nothing could pry him loose from the mechanical arm's grip.

As the robot yanked Juni away, he saw Carmen's arm dangle her over a counter that was covered with dough. It dropped her right into the middle of the flowery mess. Then, it grabbed a bowl of melted butter and poured it over her head. After dousing her with cinnamon and sugar, the arm began rolling Carmen up in the dough. She was going to be baked into a giant cinnamon roll!

"Carmen!" Juni cried. "Noooo-blub-blub-blub!"

Juni's screams went gargly when he was dumped into a giant blender filled with juice. His mechanical arm began slicing bananas over Juni's head. Next it reached for some strawberries.

In another minute, Juni thought desperately, I'm going to be a giant smoothie. I've gotta get out of this!

On the other side of the food court, Carmen was thinking: a giant cinnamon roll?! This is what I've been reduced to? I've gotta get out of this.

Then, at the same moment, each Spy Kid thought: but how?!

The spy siblings were still pondering their escape when suddenly, a glass elevator in the center of the food court opened. And from that gleaming elevator stepped—Web Pichman! In person, he looked even slicker and more plasticky than he had been on the Internet. He stalked to the middle of the food court and gazed at the butter-doused Carmen and the fruit-covered Juni. Then he unleashed a maniacal laugh.

"Now, why would anyone want to shop at such a dangerous mall," he asked the kids tauntingly, "when they can safely click in at Whoppershopper.com?"

Web reached into the pocket of his shiny suit and pulled out a digital camera.

"In fact," he added, snapping pictures of each Spy Kid, "I think this will make an excellent page on my Web site. A cautionary tale, if you will."

"I don't think you'll be posting that pic, Pichman!"

Web gasped.

Juni gasped.

Carmen gasped and blushed.

The voice belonged to Jake! Silently, he'd climbed to the top of the giant cheeseburger. Now he was gazing down at Web. And he was armed with an oversized pixie stick and a bag of jawbreakers. He was ready to attack.

"Why, hello there, little boy," Web said, gazing up at Jake. "You think you can conquer me with candy. How quaint. How very . . . mall."

"Dude," Jake said in a low growl. "Don't you dare dis the mall!"

With that, Jake lifted the pixie stick to his mouth. Both ends of the stick had been torn open.

I bet, Juni thought jealously, Mickey ate the tasty pink sugar inside.

Jake shoved a jawbreaker into the paper tube and puffed out his cheeks. Then he blew with all his might.

Twhoooop!

"Aaaggh!" Web cried as the jawbreaker thwacked him right in the forehead. Slapping his hand over his face, he stumbled backward from the pain and the force.

That's when Red and Mickey popped out from behind a candied nut cart and began covering the villain with silly string!

"Aaaaigh!" Web cried again. This time he stumbled forward, clawing at his face. But he was so wrapped up in silly string, he was blinded.

Thwooop!

Jake hit Web with another jawbreaker while Mickey and Red ran to the Spy Kids' rescue. They located OFF buttons at the base of each robotic arm. Instantly, the giant claws slackened, and Carmen and Juni were able to crawl out of their clutches.

Carmen self-consciously smoothed her greasy, cinnamon-dusted hair back. Then she looked at the mall rats and said, "How can we thank you?"

"By finding the computer hub and devirtualizing the mall," Jake yelled from atop the cheeseburger. Then he turned to pelt Web with yet another jawbreaker.

"Hurry!" Red said to Carmen and Juni. She pulled three more cans of silly string out of her pockets. "We stopped at Pincher's Gifts and Sweet-Sweet-Sweetie's candy store on the way over here. We've got plenty of ammo to hold this baddie off while you go find the computer."

"Not to mention, your mom and dad," Mickey said, shooting the Spy Kids a sympathetic glance between silly string squirts.

"Good plan," Juni said with a curt nod.

"We promise," Carmen added, "we won't let you down!"

"Later, skater!" Jake yelled, waving at Carmen with a cockeyed grin. "Good luck!"

With that, the Spy Kids made a run for it!

Carmen and Juni sprinted through the virtual mall.

"We have to find that computer hub!" Carmen huffed. "If we find the hub, we'll find Mom and Dad—I'm sure of it!

As she spoke, she leaped out of the way of a carousel horse that had jumped off the merry-too-loud. It was galloping through the mall, whinnying shrilly. The horse almost knocked her over, but Carmen recovered her balance and kept running.

As Juni huffed behind Carmen, he was nearly splattered by a Sno-Tornado, which was sort of like a giant snow cone that had come to life.

But *he* kept running.

The Spy Kids ran past garishly lit stores that sold nothing but strangely colored goggles. There were popcorn stands with nothing but burnt kernels, waterless water fountains, toyless toy stores, and recordless record stores.

And they kept running.

But when they'd gone for about a mile, Juni slowed to a stop. He looked around. Every store in the area seemed to be selling blobby, brightly glowing lava lamps. Twangy, psychedelic music throbbed through the air, making Juni's head pound and his shoulders sag. He kicked at a bright orange floor tile in frustration.

Carmen jogged to a halt, turned around, and stared at him with her hands on her hips.

"What are you waiting for?" she sputtered. "We've gotta keep looking!"

"For what?" Juni said. "How are we even going to recognize the hub if we find it? We might have run right by it! I mean, look at all this glowy stuff."

He gestured wildly at the sea of lava lamps. "*Any* of these things could be an entrance to the hub. Maybe . . . maybe Web has won!"

"Don't say that!" Carmen said. "Have you forgotten he has Mom and Dad?"

This just made Juni's head hang lower.

"No, Juni," Carmen said, stomping her foot in frustration. "You *can't* give up. We have to . . . Hey, what's going on?!"

The moment Carmen had stamped her foot on one of the orange floor tiles, the lava lamps had all disappeared! So had the crazy music. And the flashing lights!

It was all replaced by a serene garden scene. Where there had been lava lamps, there was now a sparkling pond filled with lily pads and shiny glass orbs. Butterflies flitted from flower to flower. Sweet flute music and sunshiny perfume filled the air. The nearby stores were filled with wind chimes, fragrant oils, and yoga videos. Yellow price tags fluttered from the wares like flower petals. It was peace and quiet for sale.

"How cynical," Carmen scoffed.

"How . . . weird!" Juni pointed out. "The entire setting just changed."

"Well, duh," Carmen said sullenly. "We're in a virtual environment. Things could change anytime."

"Yeah," Juni said slowly. "But that change would have to come from the computer hub. And we know Web isn't in the computer hub—he's being beamed by silly string in the food court. So . . . maybe your stomp jostled a mouse or something. But for that to be possible, the computer hub would have to be right under our feet!"

"Juni," Carmen said, her brown eyes widening. "I hate to say this, but that's brilliant!"

She spun around, looking wildly for some sort of stairwell or doorway.

"There's one!" she cried, running to a gray door tucked between two storefronts. A red exit sign glowed above the door. Carmen grabbed the knob and pulled.

And then she yanked. Nothing happened.

She pulled a lock-picking tool out of her utility belt and fiddled with the knob for five whole minutes. Finally, she almost screamed with exasperation.

"I'm not sure if this is even a real door," she cried. "It's impossible to open."

When she looked to Juni for a response, she realized he'd been ignoring her! In fact, he seemed transfixed by one of the glass orbs floating in the peaceful lily pond.

"Hello?" Carmen blurted. "C'mon, Juni. Don't go all Zen on me now. We've got big trouble! We're locked out of the hub."

"Maybe," Juni said slowly. He was scratching his head in thought. "Or maybe not," he finished philosophically.

He stood up and fished around in one of his cargo pants pockets. He pulled out his pocket-sized computer and used his wireless modem to log onto the Web.

"What are you doing?" Carmen asked. She walked up behind Juni and peeked over his shoulder. "Whoppershopper.com?! What? Are we buying from the enemy now?"

"Please," Juni said, as he pointed and clicked his way around the Web site. "I'm not gonna buy anything. I just have a hunch . . ."

Suddenly, as Juni clicked on a page within the Whoppershopper site, the computer started spewing music. It was the same twangy, psychedelic music the Spy Kids had just heard a few minutes ago! And on the screen were flashing lights and lava lamps!

Breathlessly, Juni pointed and clicked again. Now, the peaceful flute music was playing on the site, and the screen was fluttering with butterflies and lily ponds.

"I *thought* this all looked familiar!" Juni said. "The virtual environment is directly linked to Whoppershopper.com! The Web site was Web's blueprint!"

"You're right!" Carmen said. But then she frowned. "Um, how does that help us?"

"If we're somehow standing in the Web site," Juni said, his eyes lighting up, "then there must be a way to log off! We just have to find it!"

The Spy Kids began looking at the touchy-feely

stores with a fresh eye. Suddenly, Juni pointed at a sign above one of the stores.

"Look over at that store," he cried. "It's called *Alternative* Solutions. 'To help you *delete* the *shift*ing problems of life.'"

Carmen snapped her fingers. Then she glanced at the exit door—the one that had defied even her best lock-picking tools. She gasped.

"Check it out," she told her brother. "The sign over that door doesn't say 'EXIT' at all. It says 'ESCAPE'!"

"And there it is," Juni crowed. "'Alt, shift, delete'—the three buttons on the computer keyboard that will get you out of any Web site!"

Carmen gave her brother an intense look.

"Ready?" she asked him.

"Ready!"

Juni ran to stand beneath the Alternative Solutions doorway. Carmen dashed to the ESCAPE door. It still looked solid and impenetrable. She gulped. If this didn't work, she was going to have quite a lump on her head!

"One . . ." Juni called out from his perch.

"Two . . ." Carmen replied.

Finally, both the Spy Kids took deep breaths and said: "Three!"

Then they jumped. Juni hopped into the store, but he didn't land on the floor. Instead, he felt himself fall through a substance that felt sort of like wet cotton balls.

Meanwhile, Carmen plunged right through the door. *It* felt like sticky sawdust. Then she found herself plummeting down a slick slide.

"Aaaaaah . . . *Ooof*!" Juni grunted as the cotton balls finally gave way. He landed on a hard surface with a groan.

"Aaaaaaah . . . *Oh*!" Carmen cried as she flew out of the slide and skidded to a halt on a hard surface. She shook her head and looked around.

To her left, Juni was sitting on the floor. In front of her was the humming mainframe that the kids had seen on Web's computer monitors. Its lights were flashing, its bells were ringing, and its whistles were whistling.

And huddled to the kids' right, with gags of cheap, silk Whoppershopper scarves around their mouths and tacky plastic ropes around their ankles and wrists, were Mom and Dad!

"Yes!" Juni said, pumping his fist in the air. The Spy Kids clambered to their feet and ran to hug their parents. The four Cortezes were together again!

CHAPTER 14

Carmen yanked off her parents' gags.

"Oh, kids," Mom cried, giving each young spy a kiss. "We were so worried! That Web is a greedy villain."

"And he's a terrible poet," Dad sniffed. "Did you get a load of those rhymes? Pee-ew!"

"That might be the butter in my hair that you're smelling," Carmen said with a grimace. "I was this close to becoming a giant sweet roll, with a Juni smoothie on the side."

"What?!" the aghast spy parents said together.

"I'll let Juni explain while he unties you," Carmen said briskly. She leaped to her feet and raced across the room to the mainframe. "But right now, I've got a job to do."

Defiantly, Carmen plunked her cinnamon-smeared self into Web's chair and began typing away on the computer's central keyboard. Deftly, she began to chip away at the security blocks Web had installed in his computer program.

But breaking into the virtual environment wasn't going to be as easy as just decoding some password. Web had littered the program with hacker sand traps—questions that *had* to be answered correctly. One gaffe and the system would shut her out entirely.

Nervously, Carmen made her way though the first few questions. They were easy enough. "What's the capital of Zimbabwe? Name all thirty-six Inuit words for snow. If a train left Omaha at forty-five miles per hour and another train left Providence at sixty-five miles per hour, what meal would the dining cars be serving when the trains crossed paths?"

"Cinchy," Carmen said, typing her answers into the computer. She'd hacked several levels into the program when a more challenging formula popped up on the screen: "If X is to Z as C is to A, and D is inversely proportionate to H, but directly opposite of K, then what number would logically correspond to G?"

Carmen gaped at the equation and gnawed on her lower lip.

"If somebody *ever* comes up with a good reason for algebra, I want to know it," she muttered. Then she turned and glanced at her family, who were pacing nervously in front of the hub door.

"I need a little help from the big guns," Carmen announced. "Mom!"

Mom rushed over to read the problem. Then, the Cortez women started computing. As they did, Juni's spy watch buzzed.

"Hello?" Juni said into the watch's speaker.

"Dude!"

It was Jake. And he was gasping for breath!

"Hey, Juni," Jake huffed. "I've got you on my speakerphone. We're all okay. But Web's headed your way, man! We held him off as long as we could. I went through all my jawbreakers, but he didn't give up. Then he finally unraveled himself from the silly string and made a break for it."

"Tell 'em about the pizza!" Mickey's proud voice piped up in the background.

"Pizza?" Juni asked with interest.

"Yeah," Mickey replied. "When Web started running, I tossed some supergreasy pizza slices in front of him. He slid for a good ten feet. It was sweet!"

"Yeah," Red's voice piped up. "That shiny suit of his was ruined. He was superannoyed."

"Great," Dad muttered. "Now we've got a *mad,*

mad villain on our hands. How're you doing, Carmen?"

"Got it!" Carmen announced as she and Mom scribbled the last number of their equation on a piece of paper. "Four! Of course, it's so obvious!"

Triumphantly, Carmen typed in the answer.

"Correct," an electronic voice in the computer announced. "You are now entering the final decryption level before full entry. . . ."

"We're almost in," Carmen called out.

"Kewl!" Jake's voice said through Juni's spy watch. Carmen couldn't help but grin. But as Web's last question appeared on the screen, her smile faded quickly. In fact, her face fell.

"Oh, this is too much," she complained. "Listen to this: 'If a distressed pair of dirt-washed GK jeans is marked down $15, then put on the 25-percent-off sale rack, and they have a slight tear in the cuff— how much will the jeans cost?' Ack! I don't even know how to begin to solve this one."

Juni and Dad's faces were utterly blank. Even shopping-savvy Mom was flummoxed. Carmen's shoulders slumped. To have come all this way, and be blocked at the final pass! It was madden—

"Piece of red velvet cake," said a voice in Juni's spy watch. It was Red!

"Okay, the latest GK jeans? Sixty-five bucks," Red declared. "*But* what most people don't know is that the dirt-washed, distressed GKs were introduced in the third quarter of last year's fall fashion lineup. Which means, as of three days ago, they are totally out of style! So they're already worth only $58. Subtract $15 and you've got $43. Twenty-five percent off that is $32.25. And, as any savvy shopper knows, a *slight* tear is about a quarter inch long. And any tear of an inch or less means $7.50 off. That's totally standard practice."

The slack-jawed spies just nodded at Juni's spy watch in awe. If the Olympics ever launched a shopping competition, Red was a shoo-in for the American team. She was a total pro.

She rattled off the rest of her calculation without a moment's hesitation.

"And $32.25 minus $7.50 is $24.75," she said. "I'd buy 'em. That's a pretty good deal, even for last season's jeans."

"Wow," Juni breathed. "Impressive!"

Carmen typed the figure into the computer and held her breath.

The computer's bells started ringing wildly.

The whistles blew in alarm.

The mainframe shimmied and shook. Then the

lights dimmed and the computer's loud whirring died down to a feeble hum.

The Cortezes gave one another apprehensive looks.

"Uh, what just happened?" Juni asked quaveringly.

Jake answered through the cell phone.

"Dudes!" he cried. "You did it! The food court's totally back to normal. The fro-yo is frozen again. The cinnamon rolls have shrunk back down to the size of softballs. The dragon's returned to his video game, and the escalators are no longer endless!"

Juni ran to the computer hub door and threw it open. He found himself blinking in surprise at the central atrium of the mall. In the amusement park off to the left, the roller coaster and Tilt-A-Whirl were already starting to make their way around their tracks. To the right, the merry-too-loud had once again become a merry-go-round, spinning slowly to the tinkling of pretty organ music.

Shoppers were emerging from stores that once again sold ordinary items like candles, clothes, and pots and pans. They looked bleary-eyed and bedraggled, but intact.

"This end of the mall is A-OK, too!" Juni

announced to Jake. "Now all we have to do is deal with . . . Web!"

"Right," Mom said. "He'll probably be here any second. We don't have time to come up with a plan. But maybe we don't need one. After all, there are four of us and one of him."

She held her fists up in front of her face.

"I think we'll do just fine," she added grimly.

The Cortezes lined up in front of the computer hub door, their feet planted in kung fu fighting stances, and their dukes raised. They waited for the villain to return to the scene of the crime.

A minute passed.

No Web.

Another few minutes went by. Out in the atrium, several shoppers started to gather their wits and trail out of the Mall of the Universe. But a few stayed behind and resumed their shopping. In fact, it took almost no time for the mall's hum of busy consumerism to resume.

But there was still no Web!

"Surely, Web has got to be desperate to get back to the hub," Mom said in confusion. "With shoppers back in the mall, Whoppershopper.com must be losing profits with each passing minute."

"He'll be here," Dad agreed with a nod.

But after another five minutes had passed by, Mom lowered her fists to her sides.

"Web must know we're lying in wait for him," she said. "He's hiding. Which means, we've got to go find him ourselves."

"I guess that means," Juni said wearily, "it's time to hit the mall. Again!"

CHAPTER 15

As Juni rolled up his sleeves and prepared to head back into the Mall of the Universe, Carmen bit her lip.

"I think you're right," she said to her mom and brother. "But I also know computer geeks. There's only so long they can resist the lure of a warm keyboard and a glowing monitor screen. Web will come back here. I'm sure of that. So, I'm thinking . . ."

". . . we split up again?" Mom said. "Good idea. You and Juni have been all over the mall. You know it better than we do. So Dad and I will stay here and guard the hub. You go look for Web."

"Perfect plan," Carmen declared. Immediately, she and Juni plunged out into the mall. Juni gaped as he passed a family placidly licking ice-cream cones. Others were coming out of a sporting-goods store with fresh shopping bags.

"How quickly they forget that, half an hour ago,

the Mall of the Universe was, like, Dante's inferno," Juni sputtered. "They're already back to shopping till they're dropping."

"Look over there," Carmen said. She pointed to her left. "The Swiss Army knife store is really cleaning up," Carmen noted. Droves of shoppers were snapping up scissors to snip off their now useless MOTU bracelets.

"Consumers," Juni scoffed. "I just don't get i—hey!"

He stopped in his tracks and gazed with wide eyes at a store to his right.

"Check out that place," he said. He stopped to read the sign dreamily. "'View 'n' Chew—the source for all your video-watching and snacking needs.' Oooooh."

"Excuse me," Carmen said, rolling her eyes. "How quickly *you* forget—the only thing we're shopping for right now is one slick and sleazy supervillain."

"Uh, right," Juni said. He sheepishly averted his eyes from the View 'n' Chew store. "Mission first."

"Mission accomplished!"

At the sound of a gleeful, scratchy voice, Carmen and Juni spun around.

It was Red! With Jake and Mickey in tow, the

mall rats were running toward them. Red and
Mickey had silly string remnants trailing from their
shirtsleeves. And Jake's mouth was bright pink
from his pixie-stick blowgun. But other than that,
the mall rats looked like they'd survived their bat-
tle without a scratch.

When the Spy Kids and mall rats met in the middle of the atrium, they whooped and slapped each
other with high fives.

"You got us our mall back," Jake said. "You
rock!"

"Awwww," Carmen said, going beet red and
glancing shyly at her toes. She was suddenly ren-
dered speechless.

"Whatever," Juni said, rolling his eyes at his smit-
ten sister. "What Carmen is apparently too tongue-
tied to tell you is, actually, our mission is only half
over. We devirtualized the mall, but Web Pichman
is still at large. We haven't fulfilled our duties until
we've taken him into custody."

"Whoa," Jake said seriously.

"Yeah," Carmen said, recovering her voice.
"This could get sort of hairy. You guys should probably head home to safety."

"I guess," Jake said, looking at Carmen with a
flicker of worry in his blue eyes.

"Don't worry," Carmen said softly. "We're highly trained for this kind of thing. We take down villains all the time."

"Well . . ." Jake said, turning a bit pink in the cheeks himself. "Maybe I can call you later. You know . . . to make sure everything went okay?"

Now Carmen was blushing so hard, she was sure she was purple. She nodded and said weakly, "Um, yeah, call me, that'd be good. . . ."

"Whoa," Red said, staring at the scene with surprise. "Jake with a crush. Now *that's* a new one."

Jake blushed harder. Then, eager for a diversion, he pointed at a store nearby. It was one of those crowded shops that sold everything from kitchen gadgets to picture frames to stepladders. A worker had just hung a banner in the entrance that read GOING OUT OF THE MALL BUSINESS! EVERYTHING MUST GO. FIFTY PERCENT OFF, ALL DAY!

"Hey, look, Red," Jake said. "A sale. You know you can't resist a sale!"

The ploy worked. Red forgot all about teasing Jake and Carmen. She merely gave them a happy wave good-bye and headed toward the store, which was already teeming with customers. Juni stared at the shopping extravaganza and shook his head in disgust. Then he motioned to his sister.

"Well, let's keep searching," he said. He started to resume his jog through the mall, but Carmen stayed put. She was staring intently at the going-out-of-business sale. Juni doubled back to her.

"What is it?" he asked, following her gaze. Then he gasped.

A man was frantically drawing on another banner with a fat marker. The sign said FIFTY PERCENT OFF? DON'T MAKE US SCOFF! JUST GLAD TO BE ALIVE, WE'RE DOCKING SEVENTY-FIVE!

Juni drew in his breath.

"That rhyme is really bad," he said. "Bad in a familiar way . . ."

"And look at the guy," Carmen said, nodding at the sign maker. He had a paunchy, jiggly gut and a wild mane of frizzy brown curls.

"Web?" Juni said.

"Back in disguise," Carmen said, narrowing her eyes and nodding.

"So we're back in business!" Juni declared.

He started to run.

Carmen was right behind him.

In ten seconds, Juni had traversed the corridor. The supervillain was in his sights. Under his breath, Juni counted, "One . . . two . . . *three*!"

Then he jumped.

He landed squarely on Web's back.

"Ack!" the supervillain cried in surprise. "Who is that? Get him off me!"

Web began spinning in wild circles, but Juni held on to his head tightly.

"I'll get off you," he said through gritted teeth. "But I'm taking your wig with me!"

Juni dug his fingers into the villain's curls and yanked hard, but the wig didn't budge! In fact, it felt an awful lot like . . . real hair!

"Ow!" the man screeched. "What are you doing, kid?"

In surprise, Juni slid to the floor. The man spun around and faced Juni with a bewildered expression—an expression that definitely did not belong to Web D.C. Pichman.

"Whoops!" Juni said nervously. "So sorry about that, sir! Case of mistaken identity."

"First, the mall goes crazy! Now, it's the customers!" the man sputtered. He grabbed his marker and swiped an angry line through the 75 PERCENT OFF on his sign. Then he wrote, "100 percent off it all. I want out of this mall."

Cringing, Juni backed away from the angry store owner. He was about to exit the store entirely, when a voice stopped him cold.

It was coming from behind the cash register.

It belonged to a man in a long, black ponytail and a twitchy handlebar mustache.

As the man scooped armfuls of money into his cash register, he addressed the throng of sale-happy shoppers: "Hit the sale, before you bail. This might be your last chance—do the MOTU dance."

Carmen and Juni gaped at each other.

"Web!" they cried at the same time. Then together, they began running toward the cash register.

"You go for his hands," Carmen huffed to her brother. "I'll aim for the feet. Together, we'll grab him!"

But Web saw them coming. And he was ready. He planted his feet and hit them with his familiar Whoppershopper.com sales pitch: "Something that slices and dices," he snarled. "The duds that are nicest? Cures for your vices! Or how 'bout some *mices*?!"

As he said the last line, Web pulled something out from beneath the counter. It was a handful of computer mice. But these were no ordinary point-and-clickers. They were robotic mice with lots of teeth—sharp ones!

Cackling, Web tossed the mean little robots at

the Spy Kids! The mice began snapping at their shirtsleeves and hair. Carmen and Juni skidded to a halt and threw up their arms to protect themselves. While they were distracted, Web reached for a big, red button on his cash register.

He pushed it.

Swooooossh!

Suddenly, a shimmery, almost-invisible tube erupted from the middle of the shop's floor. It looked just like the snapping snouts that Carmen and Juni had fought off when they'd first arrived at the mall. It was a seam to a virtual environment!

The tube undulated threateningly, snapping at any shoppers who lurked nearby. Web ran for it. Desperately, the Spy Kids shook off the last of the snapping mice and chased after him.

The supervillain leaped at the tube. In fact, he jumped right inside it! The seam swallowed him up like a piece of candy. Then it began to turn shimmery and wavy.

"Web must have put a sudden-death fail-safe in the virtual environment program!" Carmen cried as the kids ran toward the tube. "Now that he's accessed it, that tube's going to disappear."

"Not before we take it for a little ride," Juni yelled with determination. He leaped at the tube.

It swallowed him up!

So, Carmen took a gulp and jumped, too. She made it inside the tube, just before it evaporated in a shimmer of fluttery dots.

The chase was on!

"Aaaaaah!" the Spy Kids cried. From the moment they'd leaped into the virtual reality seam, they'd been tumbling down a slick, slimy tunnel. The tunnel twisted and turned and even did a loop-de-loop.

"Ugh," Juni cried, clutching his stomach. "I'm getting tunnel sick."

"Hang in there," Carmen yelled as she slid along behind him. "It's gotta end soon. And when it does, we have to have the strength to face Web."

No sooner had the words left Carmen's mouth than Juni flew out of the tunnel with one final, queasy yell. He landed in a pile of something soft and papery. A moment later, Carmen landed next to him. When the Spy Kids shook the stars from their eyes, they looked down.

Then they gasped.

They had landed in a pile of money! In fact, a heap of cash covered the entire floor of a cavernous room. On the walls were shelves filled with skateboards, board shorts, stickers, baseball caps, messenger bags, and any other gear a trendy kid could possibly want.

To Juni, the room looked very familiar.

"I know this place," he declared. "Or should I say, this Web page. We're in another site on Whoppershopper.com."

"The skater kid page?" Carmen said, eyeing the wares with an arched eyebrow.

"Tscha!" Juni said.

On one wall was a bank of computer monitors, much like the one the Spy Kids had found in the Amazonian theme restaurant. But this time, each screen was different. One displayed the Zen garden with the glass orbs and flowers. Another was filled with lava lamps. Yet another was the very room of skater duds in which the Spy Kids were standing. Every time one of the pages racked up a sale, it emitted a loud *Cha-ching!* Then a wad of dollars spat out of a slot beneath the computers.

The room was slowly being filled with cash.

But at the same time, it was being emptied out—by Web D.C. Pichman! Still wearing his ugly black wig and mustache, the mad villain was standing on the other side of the huge room. He was scooping money off the floor and stuffing it into shopping bags.

"Let's get him!" Juni said to his sister.

Web glanced up and sneered.

"I don't think so, kiddies," he blurted. Shoving one last handful of money into his bag, Web raced for a circular doorway in the room's far wall. It looked like the mouth of another tunnel! Parked in front of it was a single, engine-powered motor scooter. Clearly, Web had set the stage for a quick getaway.

As Carmen began to run after him, Web hopped onto the scooter and fired up its engine.

"No!" Carmen cried. She began to sprint. But Juni just leaned against the wall and just watched Web go.

"What are you doing?" Carmen screeched over her shoulder. "We've got to get him."

"Why bother?" Juni said with a shrug. "He's not going anywhere."

"Huh?" Carmen blurted.

At that moment, she heard a sputter and a cough over by the tunnel. It was the motor scooter. Before it had made it ten feet, its motor had conked out!

"Blast!" Web cried. He turned over the engine

again. It barely caught, then died with another cough.

"No!" Web screamed. He started to run.

And that's when Juni joined Carmen in chasing the villain down. They caught up to him easily.

"No!" the villain shrieked again. He dropped his money bags and put up his dukes. But Web was a Web-head through and through, and he hadn't been to a gym in a long time. With only a few expert kung fu moves, the Spy Kids were able to overpower him and cuff his hands behind his back.

As Carmen jumped for joy, Juni called his parents to tell them about Web's capture.

"Good job, Junito!" Dad's voice said through Juni's spy watch. "I can see your location with my own spy locator. Just go to the end of that tunnel and you'll be in the parking lot. We'll meet you there—with an OSS car that will take Web Pichman into custody."

"No . . ." Web cried once more. He seemed to be searching for a witty retort. But clearly, he was all rhymed out. So he merely hung his bewigged head in silence as Carmen and Juni grabbed his elbows to lead him down the tunnel.

"How did you know Web wouldn't make it?"

Carmen asked her brother as they made their way through the tunnel.

"Well, unlike Web here," Juni said, "I've read the complaints and returns page of Whoppershopper.com. Those expensive scooters are the most notorious of Web's shoddy products. Every one of them makes it about five feet before petering out."

As Carmen giggled at Web's misfortune, they reached the end of the tunnel. And as promised, their proud parents were waiting for them. So was an OSS car. A couple of agents quickly grabbed Web and put him under arrest.

Carmen and Juni ran to give their parents a triumphant hug. But they could barely get near their mother. She was loaded down with shopping bags.

"Uh, go a little mall crazy, did you?" Carmen asked her mom.

Mom's green eyes crinkled up sheepishly.

"Well, you *did* need those new school clothes," she told the kids. "And there were all these great sales. Once I knew you'd saved the day, I just couldn't resist."

Dad and Juni grinned at each other and rolled their eyes.

"Women and malls," Dad said. "It's a love affair that will never die. Mark my words, my boy."

"Actually, Dad," Carmen said, glancing at the looming Mall of the Universe with a curled lip, "I think our little mission may have cured me of my mall fever. At least until the spring fashion line is released. At this point, the only thing I want to consume is a nice, simple, home-cooked dinner."

"Kewl!" Juni said in a perfect imitation of Jake's skater-kid voice. "I'm starving. Let's blow this mall and head for home. I've officially shopped till I dropped."